GLORIA WHITE'S ... RONNIE
VE... MYSTERIES

MONEY TO BURN . . .

"White at her best: fast-paced and tightly written
. . . a likable and down-to-earth character."
—*San Francisco Chronicle*

"A fast-paced adventure . . . a web of personal re-
lationships and professional intrigues that reach
into surprising crannies."
—*Publishers Weekly*

"A likable new detective . . . Ventana is complex
and charming."
—*Cape Cod Times*

. . . *AND* MURDER ON THE RUN

"Irresistible. . . . You feel [White] had a fine time
writing the book; as a result, you'll have a fine time
reading it."
—*The Plain Dealer* (Cleveland)

"A fast-paced, lively whodunit."
—*The Drood Review of Mystery*

"White shows us calamity, danger, disaster, and finally justice, through unique characters and sus-
penseful plot."
—*Mostly Murder*

CHARGED WITH GUILT

GLORIA WHITE

A DELL BOOK

Published by
Dell Publishing
a division of
Bantam Doubleday Dell Publishing Group, Inc.
1540 Broadway
New York, New York 10036

ISBN: 0-440-22049-1

Printed in the United States of America

Published simultaneously in Canada

May 1995

10   9   8   7   6   5   4   3   2   1

OPM

To Olga

Feliz cumpleaños

ACKNOWLEDGMENTS

I wish to thank the following people for sharing their expertise and their good or not-so-good experiences with me: Ellen and Sally Klages, Heidi Nigh, Barbara Wittmer, Terry Dimond, Bill Balin, and Sue Cox. For equal and infinite parts of patience and support, I'd like to thank Jackie Cantor, Vicky Bijur, and the incredible Mr. K.

CHAPTER 1

CURSING CHARLOTTE MURPHY, I raked the lock pick over the pins three more times before they finally fell into place. She'd told me to expect a Winfield lock, not a Justco. It was an easy mistake, a small one even, but it threw me off stride just the same.

I hadn't liked her or the big hurry she'd been in for me to test her security system, but Presidio Heights was a San Francisco neighborhood I hadn't worked before and word of mouth in a new territory could be good for business. Or so I'd told myself.

I hadn't turned the lock yet. I could leave now and come back another time. Or forget the whole gig altogether. But where was the profit in that?

I turned my wrist. The lock clicked, then sprang open. Shoving my way inside, I held my breath and listened for sounds above the racing of my own heart. A foghorn groaned in the distance. Inside, nothing—nothing but ticking clocks and the distant hum of a refrigerator from somewhere down the hall. Empty-house sounds.

I exhaled, blinked against the dim light, then ran my eyes in a circle around the foyer and headed for the closet. The burglar alarm control panel was most likely in there, probably set for the usual twenty-second lapse between working the lock and sounding the alarm.

I moved quickly in a rush to beat the system, swinging the door open to search for the panel's bright red LED readout. But the closet was dark. I flashed my penlight around and fought the mounting sense that something was wrong.

In the next instant I found the panel. The LED readout was dark. The burglar alarm system was already turned off. How was I supposed to compromise the system if she hadn't even turned it on?

I was busy trying to make sense out of that when something, a sound, filtered into my consciousness. Somebody . . . somebody was crying —no, *sobbing*—upstairs.

Had the sound been there earlier and I just hadn't heard it? I didn't know. What I did know was that definitely the gig was up.

I bolted from the closet, then froze in the middle of the foyer. Something had changed. Something was different. By the door. The opaque glass panel next to it. *There.* As I watched, a shadow moved behind the glass panel. Somebody was out there. The sobbing upstairs got louder. *The back. Go out the back!*

Adrenaline flooded my limbs, but for some reason I just couldn't move.

Something clicked. The front door burst open. Then a blinding light hit my eyes.

"Freeze! Police!"

I was surrounded by blue uniforms, nervous faces, and what seemed like fifty guns all pointed at me.

"Relax!" I shouted, dropping my gym bag full of tools and spreading my arms, palms out, to show I wasn't armed.

Somebody shoved me up against the wall, face to plaster, and told me not to move. I didn't. Somebody else kept the flashlight on me while the others bustled around, moving and shouting in the dark. *Why don't they turn on the lights?*

"Somebody's upstairs!" an alarmed voice shouted.

"We're clear in back, sir," somebody else said.

Another voice answered the first one, "We'll back you up the stairs. Let's go. Stevenson! Lucas! Let's go!"

The movement in the flashlighted shadows behind me seemed to go on forever. I felt like I was caught in the middle of some kind of commando action. There were shouts from upstairs, and a second wave of policemen arrived. Then suddenly everything went quiet. I turned my head to see why.

All the flashlights were pointed in one direction, at the stairs, so I looked over my other shoulder to see. One of the uniforms led a bulky and overgrown shuffling teenager down the steps. The kid was huge, bigger than the officer, and he moved with the awkward, jerky motion of somebody who doesn't quite have complete control of his limbs. His hands covered his face and he was sobbing pitifully, shoulders heaving, and short, stubby fingers digging into his eyes.

"Watch your step," the cop escorting the boy cautioned.

Why don't they just turn on the lights?

"Who's that?" somebody beside me asked.

"Gil found him in a bedroom, scared shitless. Listen"—the voice took on a low, confidential tone—"Gil thinks he's—he thinks he's retarded."

"Yeah." The tone was mildly skeptical. "He looks normal, kind of clumsy."

"Yeah. Well he's *real* slow. And his room? It looks like a kid's room—full of toys and shit. And look at the way he's cryin'." Then louder from the escort: "We got anybody to look after him?"

"Shoulda left him up there," a voice beside me said. "Post is gonna blow a gasket he finds out we moved anything."

I dropped my hands and turned around. Trying to keep the horror from my voice, I asked, "Did you say Post? Lieutenant Philly Post?"

In the glow of flashlights I could see that the cop nearest me looked Italian—hooked nose, eyes the color of a mink coat, and rich, curly black hair. He was probably the one questioning the kid's retardation.

"Turn around," he said. "Put your hands on the wall."

I did. Then I swiveled my head back and asked the black guy standing next to the Italian, "Just tell me this: Did Post transfer out of Homicide? Is he working Burglary now?"

The black cop stared back at me with one of those I'm-made-of-lead-and-you-can't-distract-me looks they teach the guys at the police academy.

"Well?" I prompted. "What's going on? Did he transfer or not?"

I refused to think Post was still in Homicide.

Somebody brought in a huge lanternlike thing that lit up the foyer and the bottom half of the stairs. Why didn't they just turn on the lights, throw the breaker switch? The black cop kept staring back at me, then finally looked away.

I lowered my arms. "Am I under arrest?"

"Get your arms up there!"

A beer-bellied officer clumped down the stairs, caught the black cop's eye, and nodded. The black cop—his name tag said *M. Tyrell*—grabbed my right wrist, swung it down from the wall to the small of my back and slapped a handcuff on it. Then he reached for my other hand.

"Hey!" I pulled away. "What are you doing? What's going on?"

He flipped his wrist and spun me around with a deftness I hadn't expected. Before I knew it, both hands were secured behind my back.

"You're under arrest—" Beer-belly began.

"For what? I—"

"You're under arrest for the the murder of Payton Lewis Murphy."

I gasped. "*Senator* Murphy?"

"You have the right to remain silent—"

"Wait! Wait! There's been some kind of mistake. I didn't—"

"Anything you say can and will . . ."

I didn't hear the rest. I didn't hear anything until a big, imposing man with hair like the mane of a lion and monster-size circles of sweat under his arms charged through the front door. Philly Post. Everybody else was wearing jackets. Not Post. He was in shirtsleeves and he was sweating like he'd just run fifty laps.

."Hey, Lieutenant," Beer-belly called out. He was across the foyer now at the foot of the stairs. Post walked over and talked to him while I weighed my options.

Post and I had worked a couple of cases together in the past and had what I thought was a fairly professional relationship. But nothing that would get me any special favors. Especially not with half the San Francisco police force milling around like a bunch of hornets.

The black cop, Tyrell, said something to Post, and Post glanced my way, then vanished upstairs for what seemed like hours. Finally the coroner's people showed up and hauled a body out in a black plastic bag.

After a bunch of shouting back and forth,

somebody threw the breaker switch. The whole house lit up in minutes as officers ran from room to room turning on the lights.

A dark East Indian woman in flowing silk who I hadn't seen arrive walked with an ambulance crew as they hustled the sobbing retarded guy out on a stretcher. He never looked at me and I never saw his face.

"Ms. Ventana." Officer Tyrell took my arm and led me into the living room.

Post was standing alone by the empty fireplace, amid what was probably a few hundred thousand dollars' worth of antique French furniture. No wonder they wanted their burglar alarm tested.

As soon as Tyrell left, Post motioned me to sit. I turned and lifted my handcuffed wrists. "What about these?"

The door opened, and Kendall, Post's obsequious assistant, walked in. He nodded at Post, closed the door, then glanced at me, dipping his head in what I guess was his version of hello.

I nodded back, then turned to Post, handcuffed wrists still in the air. "How about it?"

"Sit down, Ventana."

"Come on, Post. What do you think I'm going to do, bolt for the door the minute you take the cuffs off? Have you ever worn these things? They're doing something awful to my wrists."

"Sit down."

His attitude was more brusque than usual. Not a good sign. I took his cue and sort of slouched into a chair, crushing my arms behind me. I didn't care—I was tired of standing.

Kendall pulled a tiny notebook and a pencil out of nowhere and waited.

"All right, Ventana." Post's voice was weary. Too weary for—I glanced at the ornate clock on the mantel—two o'clock in the morning. I'd been the one standing in the foyer for the last hour and a half. "What's the story?"

I opened my mouth but the echo of my lawyer's angry voice made me close it. Phoebe Wright, who I think after five years was starting to get fed up with my unique approach to the security business, had complained violently the last time I'd gotten caught breaking into a place up in Tiburon. She'd said she had to work twice as hard to undo all the damage I'd done by trying to talk myself out of jail. According to her, that's why I'd been denied bail.

But this was Philly Post. I *knew* Philly Post. I hadn't known that other creep.

I looked up into Philly Post's unreadable face and took a deep breath.

"Well?" he demanded. "What are you doing here?"

Kendall stood in the corner, pencil poised, his narrow face expressionless. I took another deep breath.

"I was testing their burglar alarm," I said.

Post snorted. "You broke in."

"I was *invited* to break in. I've got a signed release. It's right here in my pocket." Phoebe had insisted I use the one-sheet form she'd drafted after the time up in Tiburon.

Post nodded at Kendall, who came toward me. I gestured with my chin toward my jacket's breast pocket.

A blushing Kendall reached delicately inside, but his hand came out empty. That's when I remembered I'd run out of copies and forgotten to bring the release to my meeting with Charlotte Murphy.

I looked up. Post was staring sourly at Kendall's empty hand. Slowly his eyes shifted toward mine.

"All right, Ventana," he said, and his voice echoed off the rich antiques like doomsday. "I think you'd better come downtown."

CHAPTER

2

"DIDN'T I TELL YOU not to talk to the cops without me?"

Phoebe Wright didn't even bother to say hello when the matron brought me into the interview room. She just burst out of her chair and started chewing me out.

Since I'd just spent the past forty-five minutes sitting alone in a holding cell wondering how come Charlotte Murphy hadn't mentioned that her husband was Payton Murphy, the senator, and why hadn't I figured it out myself, I wasn't in the mood to hear Phoebe or anybody else for that matter tell me I'd messed up. She paused for breath and I looked at her.

Her silk blouse and blue wool suit were wrinkled and her mind-of-its-own curly blond hair stuck out in every direction. There were faint pillow scars on her left cheek and, naturally, since it was five o'clock in the morning, she looked like she just woke up.

My irritation melted. I felt bad, like I usually do when I see her, for getting into trouble and for getting her out of bed one more time. There was no way around her sleepy but earnest anger.

"I know Post," I said after she'd finally wound herself down.

"Doesn't matter. He'll still testify against you. It's his job."

"I told him the truth, Phoebe. I was hired to break in."

She sighed, pulled out a notebook and a fountain pen from her open-topped satchel, and took the chair opposite mine.

"You've got to come up with a better sideline than this, Ronnie. If you ever paid me, you'd realize you're barely breaking even. Did you at least show Post the release?"

"Uh—well . . ."

"Ronnie? The release I drafted for you. You've been using it, haven't you?"

"Well . . . I kind of forgot to get her to sign it."

Phoebe tossed her pen on the table and threw her hands up in the air. "I give up. What did I tell you about getting a signed release? It indemnifies you. These people not only think you broke into Payton Murphy's house, they think you killed him. It would have been nice to show you had"—she coughed—"legitimate business there."

No sense lingering over that sore spot. "You're right," I said. "You're absolutely right. How did Murphy die?"

Phoebe paused just long enough to let me know she knew I was changing the subject. "He was electrocuted."

"Electrocuted! This is crazy. Has anybody thought this through? Why am I going to break into somebody's house—a complete stranger's house—and electrocute him?"

Phoebe's jaw dropped. "You didn't know him?"

"Of course not. I've *heard* of Senator Murphy, but I never met him."

"Who hired you, then?"

"His wife. Look, what was he doing? How was he electrocuted?"

Phoebe hesitated. "A radio in the bathtub."

"*A radio in the tub?* That could have been an accident. Why do they think I killed him? Why do they think *anybody* killed him?"

"You know how cops think: You were there."

"But I was *supposed* to be there."

Phoebe's lips formed a thin line. "You're going to need a tighter defense than that, Ronnie."

"Who tipped the police?"

"They got an anonymous call reporting a burglary from a phone booth down the street. If it weren't for that, if no one had seen you go in, they'd probably be calling it suicide. Or an accident."

Not an accident. Not suicide. Murder. I remembered the clunky retarded teenager they'd brought down from the second floor.

"What about the guy upstairs?"

Phoebe perked up. "What guy?"

"He was up there crying when I broke in. It must have been him. I didn't get to see him real well, but he was in his late teens. He acted younger, though, and one of the policemen said he was real slow. They brought him downstairs and hauled him off in an ambulance. There was some East Indian woman with him. He sounds like a prime suspect to me if it's got to be murder. Aren't something like ninety percent of all murder victims killed by people they know? I never met Payton Murphy, and this guy was in his house, upstairs. Even if he didn't kill Payton Murphy, he must have seen who did."

"The police didn't mention anybody else," she said.

"I saw him. They brought him downstairs."

She made a couple of notes on the pad in front of her. As she wrote, I asked, "What about Charlotte Murphy?"

Phoebe looked up. "Who?"

"Charlotte Murphy. She's the one who hired me to break in."

Phoebe kept writing in her notebook. When she looked up again, she didn't seem as upset with me.

"Start at the beginning," she said.

"I got there around ten—"

"No. I mean when did you meet Charlotte Murphy? Start then."

"She called me last week and said she'd heard about me from Frankie Zola."

Phoebe scowled. "You *know* Frankie Zola? He's got mob ties, Ronnie."

"He was a friend of my dad's. Uncle Frankie. I haven't talked to him in years, but he was good to me when my parents died. I stayed at his house for a while before my grandmother came back from Mexico to take care of me."

"I don't think we need to bring this out at the bail hearing." Phoebe chewed on her pen and thought a minute. "You know, it really would have been nice to have that release."

No point dwelling on something I couldn't change. "I met her down at the Pied Piper, you know, at the Palace. I didn't like her, but she checked out okay. I mean, she looked all right— well dressed, not nervous, bought me lunch, and she showed me her driver's license and everything. So when I called Frankie and found out he was out of town just like she'd said, I figured I'd do it."

"Did you tell her when you planned to break in?"

"I usually give them a ballpark area but I don't tell them if I'm going in during the daytime or at night. I like to give them a general idea, though, just so I don't surprise somebody and get shot or something."

"I wish you'd listen to your husband."

"Ex. And he's remarried now, Phoebe, so let's not get into it."

Phoebe looked disappointed. She'd always liked Mitch, thought he was a good influence on me because he was constantly harping on me about getting a normal job—something in an office, at a desk, pushing papers around.

"What did you tell Mrs. Murphy about when you'd test her alarm? Specifically."

I thought back to the conversation I'd had with her. "I think I said Monday or Tuesday. She seemed in kind of a hurry. Are they bringing her in? Have they talked to her? All this is going to get cleared up once they talk to her."

"They didn't even mention her."

"And they didn't tell you about the guy upstairs either? Aren't they supposed to tell you what they've done?"

"No. All right." She capped her pen and slid it and the legal pad into her briefcase. Then she clasped her hands and rested them on the table between us. "I think we can get you bail as long as you keep quiet about Frankie Zola. Their case is all circumstantial so far. You just happened to be in the wrong place at the wrong time." It sounded like she was trying to convince herself.

"Listen, Phoebe, I think Post brought me in because he felt he had to. There were a lot of other cops around and he couldn't just let me go right there. I don't think he's going to carry this thing through," I said. "He's fundamentally a decent guy."

"That's too bad."

"Why?"

"Because you're not dealing with Post anymore. You've got Scotch Morgan."

"Who's Scotch Morgan?"

"The assistant D.A. in charge of homicides. He's out for blood, Ronnie. He smells a promotion and you're it."

CHAPTER 3

I THOUGHT THEY HAD a pretty sloppy case and, when we got to the arraignment Thursday morning, it seemed everybody agreed with me.

They left me standing at the table just inside the courtroom railing and huddled with the judge for what seemed like a long time but really must have been just a couple of minutes. Then everybody walked away, including Phoebe, while the judge muttered something I didn't understand.

When they were done, Phoebe took my elbow and hurried me toward the door like she thought the judge might change his mind.

"What happened?" I whispered.

"They're not pressing charges yet."

"Yet? You mean they still might?"

We cleared the courtroom door, but Phoebe didn't stop. She didn't let go of my elbow either. "You can't leave town and you've got to keep them posted on your whereabouts at all times. Do you understand?''

"Why? Haven't they talked to Charlotte Murphy?"

Phoebe shook her head.

"Why aren't they dropping the whole thing?"

"The witness—"

"What witness?" I asked.

"Your sobbing person? Upstairs? *That* witness. He *is* mentally retarded, and his doctor has had to sedate him. So he can't talk to anybody. The police are going to wait for him to stabilize before they question him."

"How retarded is he?"

"I don't know."

"Is he bright enough to kill somebody?"

"They're not even considering that."

"Why not?"

"No mileage," Phoebe said.

"What?"

"Politically. Scotch Morgan will get a lot farther bringing down the Ventana cat-burglar legacy than prosecuting a retarded teenager. As far as they're concerned, he's their star witness." Phoebe stopped and bit her lip. "Ronnie—"

"Don't worry. He didn't see anything. At least he didn't see me."

"Hey, Phoebe! Wait up." Scotch Morgan hurried to catch up with us.

He was a young, crisp bulldog of a guy with tight little eyes and jowls somebody that young didn't deserve. My guess was he was a handful of years out of law school and eager to climb the money ladder.

"Got a minute, Counselor?" he asked in a voice that was a pitch higher than you'd expect from such a sturdy-looking guy.

Phoebe hesitated, then turned to me. "Will you excuse me a minute, Ronnie?"

They huddled against the wall for a couple of minutes, gesturing and hissing at each other. Then Phoebe left him and came back to me.

"Scotch Morgan wants to talk to you," she said. "As your counsel, I advise you not to."

"Why does he want to talk to me?"

"Because he's got a weak case and he knows it. He thinks you'll help him out. He's fishing, Ronnie."

I glanced across the hall at eager, stuffed-into-his-suit Scotch Morgan. Maybe he just wanted to clear things up once and for all. Maybe, if he heard what I had to say, he'd drop the charges.

Phoebe shifted her weight and brought her face into my line of vision.

"I know what you're thinking, Ronnie, but he's *not* going to drop this thing. We're talking about the death of a state senator. He knows about your parents being cat burglars who never got caught. He thinks he's prosecuting them, not you. The press value here will get him a lot of mileage. Why do you think he's going after you instead of the retarded boy? He's a hot dog. It usually takes seven or eight years to make A.D.A. in charge of homicides. He joined the D.A.'s office three years ago. He's probably already daydreaming about being appointed head prosecutor for the county. Listen to me, Ronnie. He's not even supposed to talk to you. Post should."

I looked over at Morgan again. He was smiling, trying his best to look encouraging and receptive. "I'll talk to him."

Phoebe frowned. "You don't have to."

"I know. Let's do it."

Phoebe refused to go to his office—something about neutral ground being better—so we found a secluded table in a dank corner of the Hall of Justice basement cafeteria. The place smelled of fried food and bug spray.

Scotch let out a little grunt as he settled into a plastic chair across from us. He smiled and, up close, it looked like his face was going to burst.

"I appreciate your agreeing to cooperate, Ms. Ventana. I know you're probably very tired after all you've—"

Phoebe interrupted. "Cut to the chase, Scotch. What do you want?"

Annoyance flickered across his face, but he smiled. "I'd like to hear Ms. Ventana's version of what happened."

Phoebe reached for her briefcase. "Come on, Ronnie. We don't have to put up with this bull- shit."

"Bullshit! Come on, Counselor. I just want to—"

"She gave a statement already, Scotch. If you want to talk to her, you can call my office to schedule a time after my client's had some rest. Come on, Ronnie."

"But—" He looked bewildered, like she'd slapped him before he'd had a chance to make a pass.

Phoebe pushed her chair back. The hollow sound of its legs scraping against the cement floor filled the room. "Come on, Ronnie."

I didn't move. "I'd rather tell him," I said.

Phoebe glowered. Through gritted teeth, she said, "You don't have to say anything, Ronnie. In fact I advise you not to."

"I know."

Phoebe's shoulders slumped. She slapped her briefcase back down on the floor and dropped into her chair again. Scotch Morgan beamed at me.

"I'm a private detective," I began. "And on the side I test burglar alarms. I test them by breaking into places."

Phoebe kicked me under the table so I scooted my chair away from hers and continued.

"That seems to be the best way to convince people they need to improve their security."

Phoebe was glaring at me, but Scotch was happy. He was the picture of attentiveness, nodding, encouraging me to go on, his pen and paper forgotten on the table between us.

"This was just one more job I was hired to do. Mrs. Murphy—"

Scotch tilted his head to one side like the RCA Victor dog. "Who?"

"Charlotte Murphy—she's the one who hired me. Didn't Philly Post tell you? As soon as you talk to her, this'll all get cleared up. She gave me a two-hundred-dollar deposit."

"A check?"

I hesitated. Cash was something else Phoebe had told me not to do. *Get a check from them, a check and the signed release,* she'd said, *and you'll never have a problem.* "She paid cash."

Beside me Phoebe winced. Scotch Morgan nodded, then cleared his throat.

"Did this Charlotte Murphy tell you who she was? Did she mention the Senator?"

"No. I didn't even know it was the Senator's house until the police told me."

"Don't you check your clients out?"

Phoebe stiffened. "That's enough. Don't answer anything else, Ronnie. Please. Let's just go."

Morgan raised his eyebrows. I took advantage of his silence to ask, "Why hasn't anybody talked to Mrs. Murphy yet?"

He muttered something unintelligible and started stuffing his papers into his briefcase like he was ready to go.

"Who was the guy upstairs?" I asked.

Morgan looked at his watch, pushed his chair back, but stayed in it. Phoebe smiled. "She asked you a question," she said.

Morgan feigned confusion.

"The guy upstairs," I repeated.

"Do you mean Senator Murphy?"

"No. I mean the guy who was crying upstairs.

The retarded guy. Your witness. I heard him up there sobbing. Who is he? What's his name? Why isn't he a suspect?"

"He's a family member."

Phoebe and I waited.

Morgan fidgeted, drumming his fingers on the side of his briefcase. Finally he said, "He's the Senator's grandson."

"Why don't the police think *he* killed Senator Murphy instead of me? I didn't even know Payton Murphy."

Morgan hesitated again. If he didn't think he was going to get any more out of me, he would have left already. He wouldn't have answered anything else. Instead he said, "Murphy's grandson is too distressed to talk. His doctor's got him sedated, says he's had such a shock he can't even talk right now."

My heart quickened. "That could mean a lot of different things, Mr. Morgan. It could mean that he killed Payton Murphy himself. Or it could mean he saw who did."

Morgan shook his head. "Not necessarily." He cleared his throat again, settled back into his chair, and said, "Let's go back to your Mrs. Murphy. What did she look like?"

"About an inch or so taller than me, so say five-six, about one-thirty, maybe one-forty, green eyes, dark hair, tiny, turned-up nose, pierced ears and expensive-looking clothes. Early to mid thirties. Look, why don't you just talk to her? She'll tell you the same thing I've told you. She'll explain it all.''

He asked me a bunch more questions, like how I got into the place, did I use the front or the back or the side door, why did I go upstairs, and a whole series of questions based on his assumption of how things happened.

Over Phoebe's growingly rabid objections I tried to fill him in on the truth, but after a while I figured out why Phoebe didn't want me to talk to him. He had a one-track mind and his own idea of reality.

"I think this whole thing will be cleared up when you talk to Mrs. Murphy," I repeated for the hundredth time.

"That's going to be kind of hard to do, Ms. Ventana." Scotch Morgan's voice took on a slick, patronizing tone. He stopped smiling and his beady little eyes suddenly turned feral.

"You see, the Senator's wife, Charlotte Murphy? The woman you claim hired you? She died last year.''

CHAPTER

4

"FUCKIN' RINGER, HUH?"

My best friend, Blackie Coogan, stubbed out his cigarette in the ashtray protruding from the dash, blew the last of the smoke he'd inhaled out the car window, and shook his grizzled head in empathetic disgust.

His sixty-five-year-old ex-boxer's body seemed cramped in the passenger seat of my old '77 blue Toyota, but mostly Blackie just looked cool. Strike-you-blind-beautiful blue eyes, gray hair that never looked barbered but was always just the right length, a sexy smile, and a tough-guy, I-don't-give-a-shit-about-the-world attitude that made every woman drool.

I'd thought about making a pass at him once, early on when he'd first started showing me the ropes on being a P.I., but he must have read my mind because he'd muttered something about business and pleasure being like water and oil. Then he'd gone ahead and told me about the

value of bringing empty milk cartons along on a
stakeout.

I'd spent the best part of the day after Phoebe
dropped me off trying to track down the fake
Charlotte Murphy. Nobody at the Palace—the
place where alias Charlotte Murphy and I had
lunched—remembered her, and after checking
every parking garage in a four-block radius and
getting dead-ended at each one, I went home and
slept until Blackie had showed up at my door.

I turned the car onto Broadway and accelerated. Blackie glanced across at me. "So what's
your cousin, Myra, gonna do for us, doll?"

"That woman, the one claiming to be Charlotte Murphy, oozed society and money. You can't
fake something like that. At least I don't think
you can. And Myra runs with those society types. I
thought maybe if I described this person to Myra,
she'd know who I was talking about."

"Fuckin' connected, huh?"

I shrugged. "We'll see."

Myra had met Blackie once before, and she'd
been so thoroughly infatuated with him that
she'd been reduced to mincing smiles and gig-
gles. I'd forgotten about that until Blackie and I
walked into her Pacific Heights apartment and
her eyes melted.

She was barefoot in a yellow terry-cloth robe
with her face fully made up. Obviously she'd been
getting ready to go out, but she didn't mention a
word about being in a hurry. Blackie—his mere
presence—had her mesmerized.

I spent the next half hour watching her flip her flyaway blond hair off her brow while she pretended to listen to what I had to say. She never once took her eyes off Blackie. Mr. Sex Appeal. Great.

"Did you hear what I said, Myra?"

She smiled at Blackie. "Sure. They arrested you for Payton Murphy's murder and you're out on bail."

"They haven't charged me yet so I'm *not* out on bail. Besides, I covered that the first five minutes we were here. What I want to know is, have you ever seen the woman I just described?"

"What woman?"

Blackie caught my eye and winked, then turned back to Myra. Her hand played absently with the collar of her robe.

"Five-six," Blackie began, repeating what I'd just gone over earlier. "One-thirty, maybe one-forty, dark hair, green eyes, turned-up nose, spends a lot on what she wears. Early to mid thirties."

Myra giggled.

"This is important, Myra." It came out sounding too stern, but I didn't need to worry. Myra wasn't even on the same planet.

Blackie grinned, and Myra just dissolved.

"Your cousin needs a hand," he said to her.

Myra finally tore her eyes off Blackie and looked at me. I guess I looked as furious as I felt because she sobered instantly and seemed to focus for the first time since we'd walked in.

"I'm sorry, Ronnie. I really am. Tell me what's wrong."

I went through everything all over again and finished with "Does she sound like anybody you might know?"

"Sure."

My heart stopped. "Who?"

"I don't know. You've just described half the people in the Old Maids Club."

"The what?"

She blushed, mainly for Blackie's benefit. "I've told you about this social club before, Ronnie, but you never want to join. You ought to think about it. It's a group of us single girls—the top age limit is forty—and we get together and give bashes with the Swains—the single guys. Fund-raisers. Couples can come, but mostly it's a mixer."

I remembered my mother telling me about those social clubs, how the guys were all dull and self-absorbed and what an impression my father had made when he brazenly but gently broadsided her car and pretended it was an accident just so he could meet her.

"When's the next one?" I asked.

Myra grinned at Blackie so enthusiastically she almost fell out of her chair.

"Tonight," she said. "Want to come?"

CHAPTER

5

"THIS IS PRETTY USELESS," I said to Blackie, feeling battered from fighting my way through the dancing mess of people. It had taken us an hour to circle the dance floor once, making our way through the throbbing mass without seeing anybody who looked even close to Charlotte Murphy. "Let's go find Myra and tell her we're leaving."

Blackie paused. A pert brunette who looked all of thirteen, in a skirt the size of a Band-Aid, appeared in front of him.

"Will you dance with me?" she asked breathlessly.

Blackie grinned, and I thought the girl was going to collapse.

"Go ahead, Blackie. I'll catch up with you later."

As soon as Blackie vanished, a couple of guys invited me to dance. I did, mostly using the time to describe Charlotte Murphy and to ask if they knew anybody who looked like her. The first guy said she sounded like his cousin, Melva Buffing-ton, but when I grilled him some more, I found out Melva lived half the year in Nice, and this was the half she was there.

The second Swain told me I was describing his mother. "No, no. The woman I'm looking for is in her early thirties," I explained.

"Mother looks that young," he said in a voice full of admiration. "She's stunningly beautiful."

I wasn't going to argue. I wasn't going to give him my phone number either.

When I finally caught up with Myra, she was talking to a couple. The man had his back to me, but the woman didn't. I'd seen her before—once when I was at Myra's apartment she'd shown up with a black eye barely hidden by makeup and sunglasses.

"Hi, Ronnie!" Myra shouted over the music. "Have you met Casa Strand? We went to high school together. Casa, this is my cousin, Ronnie. And Dwight says he knows you, Ronnie. Do you remember him?"

The man turned toward me and, at the sight of his face, I recoiled. Dwight Baker. Ex-con. Ex-pa-rolee. He'd stared me down a zillion times from across my desk when I worked at the parole office nine years ago.

His rugged, outdoorsy good looks disguised a rough and violent psychopath who hated women almost as much as he hated himself. He'd been paroled after serving six years of a fourteen-year sentence for rape and attempted murder. His high school sweetheart had been the one who pressed charges.

I looked at Casa, clinging to his arm like he was some kind of prize. Dwight smiled that same impudent smile he'd used on me at the parole office and ran all his words together like he had back then.

"How-are-you-doing-Ronnie?-Fine?-Long-time."

I nodded. "Casa. Dwight."

"How-long's-it-been? Nine years? Yeah, nine years since you fucked me over." Dwight Baker snickered. "Too bad about Danner, huh?"

"Who's Danner?" Casa asked.

Dwight smirked. "Mutual acquaintance, wouldn't you say, Ronnie?"

Before I could answer, somebody came up and asked Myra to dance. As soon as she was gone, Dwight turned to Casa and said, "Get me a drink, baby."

She lingered a split second, long enough to cast a jealous warning glance at me, then dove into the crowd like a kid on an errand that was going to earn her ten bucks.

I turned back to the sneering bully beside me. "Still beat your girlfriends, Dwight?"

"Hey! You're not my P.O. anymore, *Ms.* Ventana. You know what I've got to say to you: It's none of your fucking business what I do with my women. But if you want a taste firsthand, if you're curious about what you're missing . . ." He ran his tongue over his lips and reached a finger toward my cheek. I batted it away before he could touch me.

He laughed like he thought I'd done something funny. "Your cute little cousin tells me you ran into some real trouble Tuesday night. Murder's a tough rap, *Ms.* P.O. I heard you could be up on murder charges and I thought to myself, 'Well, well, that's just too bad.' You got all my sympathy, P.O. honey. I know what it's like to have the law breathing down *my* neck, now, don't I?"

He let his eyes play up and down my body, slowly, pointedly, letting them linger in the right spots just long enough to make me feel threatened and uncomfortable. It was a move he'd perfected a long time ago and it worked. Instinct told me to shrink away, but I forced myself to step forward and lean in toward him, putting my face inches from his. "You haven't changed, Dwight, have you?"

It wasn't the reaction he'd expected. He sort of backed away. Then he snickered just like he'd done so often at the parole office and moved in close, close enough for me to smell his beery breath.

"I hope they fry you, bitch," he whispered with a smile, then vanished into the crowd before I could speak.

Somebody touched my shoulder and I jumped. It was Myra. "I wish Casa wouldn't date him," she said. "He gives me the creeps."

We found an empty table by the wall and ordered an Anchor Steam for me and a martini for Myra. Over the pounding music I said, "Have you talked to Casa about him?"

"Oh, sure. She doesn't care."

"Does she know he raped and tried to kill his steady girlfriend nine years ago?"

Myra gasped. "*Did* he? How do you know that?"

"He used to be one of my parolees."

"He's been in *prison*? Ugh. I don't think Casa knows that. I don't think she'd be with him if she did."

"Then tell her. He's a powder keg. If you can talk to her, you should." I remembered her bruised face from the time she showed up at Myra's. "Give her the number of a battered-women's shelter too. Tell her to memorize it. She's going to need it."

Our drinks arrived and I glanced around the room while I sipped my Anchor Steam. Blackie was discoing his brains out on the dance floor, dancing with two debs at once. Dwight Baker and Casa Strand were dancing too. Everybody was smiling, having fun, but Myra looked grim. She couldn't take her eyes off Baker.

"Is that why you quit the parole office?" she asked. "Because of guys like him?"

I took a long, slow sip of beer. "I could handle the creeps. It was the good ones I had trouble with."

Myra frowned. "The good ones? What do you mean?"

The music stopped and the band announced a ten-minute break.

"The man Baker mentioned, Joe Danner? He's why I quit. And Dwight Baker knows it."

"Danner was a reporter, wasn't he?"

I must have looked surprised because she added, "Mom told me about him."

High-fashion Aunt Emily had never talked about anything deeper or heavier than which fork to use for shrimp. "What did she say?"

"That he was a reporter and that he killed somebody when he was in jail."

"Did she mention he was in jail because he wouldn't reveal his source and the judge found him in contempt? Did she tell you the D.A. couldn't make the case without Danner? Did she say the guy who testified Danner knifed that prisoner had all charges against him dropped the day after he testified? Did she tell you that?"

Myra shook her head.

"Joe Danner was innocent," I continued. "But he served six years before the state paroled him. That's when I met him. He was a good guy, but prison messed him up and made him hard. He violated his parole after he'd been out a month. I would have let it go, but a jerk in the office found out and made a federal case out of it. I refused to send Danner back to jail, so the jerk took it over my head, past my supervisor to the Board of Prison Terms. Danner went back to serve six more months. On month number five he killed somebody. The state gave him thirty years. He was defending himself from an assault, an assault that never would have happened if he hadn't been sent back."

"Oh." Myra's voice was small, and I realized I'd raised my own voice. People were staring.

"The guy's life was ruined—twice," I explained in a softer tone. "Because the bureaucracy wouldn't leave him alone."

"Couldn't you do something?"

"I tried. I tried for six months and didn't get him a thing. That's when I quit."

I took a deep breath and looked around. People had stopped staring but I suddenly felt uneasy. Maybe it was thinking about Joe Danner all over again, or maybe it was sitting here watching the young elite of San Francisco while a murder charge hung over my head. Whatever it was wasn't going to go away.

I stood. "Tell Blackie I had to leave, will you?"

Myra's eyes widened. "But—"

"She's not here, Myra. And I can't stay."

CHAPTER

6

PEOPLE SAY DREAMS restore your mind. For me sometimes they do more than that. I woke up Friday morning remembering Charlotte Murphy's scarf.

It was blue and orange and yellow and green, sort of filmy and pastel. But the part that hit me, the part that actually woke me from my dream, was the writing on the scarf. The word SIVEN had been printed all over it in flowing, scripted letters stamped in gold.

"Oh, no, we don't sell Siven products here," the coolly elegant salesgirl at Manion's announced. "We carry Hermès. And Armani. And these Nina Riccis over here just came in yesterday."

A couple of stores later I finally got a salesclerk who wasn't into hard sell. He told me the only place I could pick up a Siven scarf in San Francisco was at a Maiden Lane shop called Montague's Trap and Saddle.

No way would I have figured that one out by

myself, so I decided to buy something just to show my gratitude. But after he showed me a blouse with a six-hundred-dollar price tag, I decided I wasn't *that* grateful.

Montague's Trap and Saddle didn't sell traps or saddles or much of anything else, for that matter. It was one of those tiny boutiques that lays out three or four items on a few tables and leaves the rest to your imagination. Lots of open space that any other merchant not selling prestige or attitude would fill with merchandise. I wondered if they had more clothes in the back, or if their stock was limited to the stuff out here.

A thin male salesclerk was busy ignoring me from the corner, so I wandered around for a minute, long enough to make sure I didn't see what I was looking for.

"Excuse me," I said.

The clerk turned my way, gave me a half-thawed look that said he forgave me this time for not wearing designer clothes, but it had better not happen again.

"My name is Cedric," he announced.

"Do you sell Siven scarves, Cedric?"

Jekyll vanquished Hyde. Cedric's icy reserve melted. He smiled at me like I was his best friend.

"A lovely choice," he said warmly, then vanished into the back room before I could say more. He came out a second later with three boxes and opened each one with a flourish. The last scarf he showed me was the same style "Charlotte Murphy" had worn.

"That one," I said. "Have you sold that one to anybody recently?"

Cedric looked at me like he didn't understand. "I beg your pardon?"

"I need to find a person who bought a scarf just like that one."

His tapered fingers absently caressed the filmy scarf. He kept smiling, but his confusion won out. "I'm afraid I don't understand."

I reached into my suddenly shabby handbag and showed him my P.I. license. What was left of his smile vanished. He recoiled in horror and started furiously stuffing the scarves back into their boxes.

"She's got dark hair," I said. "Strong features with a turned-up nose." I described the woman who had hired me, giving him details he might have remembered. "Did you sell a scarf lately to anybody who looks like that?"

Cedric grabbed the boxes and drew himself up haughtily. "I'm not in the habit of informing on my customers, Miss—Miss—"

"Ventana." I set one of my cards on the counter in front of him just as a woman popped out of the back, smiling and brandishing a hanger that held a filmy blouse with lace panels.

Why do they call this place Trap and Saddle? I wondered. She took one look at us, then froze.

"What about you?" I asked. "Have you sold any Siven scarves lately?"

Before she could answer, Cedric cut her off.

"Of course she hasn't. Now, please leave, or I'll have to telephone the authorities."

The woman salesclerk retreated a step but kept her eyes on me. Her rising curiosity wasn't lost on Cedric.

"I'll take that," he said, setting the boxed scarves down and yanking the hanger from her hand. "Finish what you were doing in the back."

"But—"

"*Finish* what you were doing in back, Katherine."

"Yes, Mr. Cedric."

As soon as she was gone, he dropped the blouse on top of the boxes on the counter and skewered me with his eyes again. "Shall I call the authorities?"

"The woman I'm looking for is involved in a murder," I said. "You can talk to me or you can talk to the police. It's up to you. Only *I* don't have any interest in her accomplices. The police might."

"Very well, then. I'd rather speak to the police. I'm sure they'll contact me if they wish. I have nothing to hide. There's no reason for anyone to suspect me or my staff of being accomplices in anything but good taste and high fashion."

Brother. I left him with his high-fashion nose in the air and drove straight to the Hall of Justice.

"A scarf?" Philly Post didn't even bother to hide his contempt. "You want us to subpoena this guy over a scarf?"

"The woman claiming to be Charlotte Murphy

was wearing a Siven scarf, Post. And Montague's Trap and Saddle is the only place in town she can get one."

"So what's this guy going to tell me?"

I took a deep breath. "You call him in, I describe the woman who hired me, and we ask him which of his customers fits that description."

"Right."

"Well, why not?"

He was silent, staring through the glass at the bustling squad room just outside his office. Then he splayed his fingers out on the untidy desk in front of him and raised his eyes to meet mine. "The way this works, Ventana, is, you're it. You're the suspect."

"Why would I kill Senator Murphy? Why would I kill *anybody*? I do B-and-Es, Post. Legal ones. I don't do murder."

Post scowled. "You're talking to the wrong stiff. Scotch Morgan's in charge."

"You're still a cop, aren't you?"

"I can't subpoena shit without Morgan's okay. I'm telling you I can't help you."

"Talk to Morgan, then. He thinks I killed Murphy."

"Nobody else is breaking down the doors asking for the honor."

"What about the grandson?"

Post shook his head. "You were caught red-handed."

"Red-handed would have been the radio flying out of my hands into the water, Post. The guy was already dead when I got there. I didn't even go upstairs. I didn't even know whose house it was."

Post leaned back in his chair and rubbed his neck. He looked tired. "You ought to check out your clients a little better, Ventana. Especially if you're going to keep breaking into places for a living. Didn't I say this was going to happen?"

I stared at him, wondering for a crazy minute if he'd been the one to set me up. Then I shrugged off the notion. Why would Post want to kill Payton Murphy?

"You said I'd get caught breaking and entering, Post. You never said a word about getting framed for murder. Look," I said, rising from the hard wooden chair. "If you change your mind and want to check out the scarf angle, I'll be happy to work with you. We could—"

Post stared at me like I'd lost my mind. Maybe I had. "You're the only game in town, Ventana. I'm not giving you squat."

I leaned in, hands resting on a cleared spot on the corner of his cluttered desk. "Tell me this, Post. If my parents had been schoolteachers instead of cat burglars, would you still be so unwilling to help me prove I didn't commit this crime?"

He stared hard into my face, not giving anything away.

"Well?" I demanded.

"Like I said, Ventana. You're the only game in town."

CHAPTER

7

I WAS SO TICKED off that I was fifteen blocks away before I remembered I had intended to stop by and see Aldo Stivick, my other police connection, the one who loves me, the one I went to high school with, the one I wish worked in Homicide. I pulled over and found a pay phone.

"Aldo? Hi, it's me, Ronnie."

"Ronnie!" His police-administration monotone took on some life and—I hated to admit it—pleasure.

"How are you?" he asked. "I was just thinking about you. I heard you were arrested Tuesday night."

"Word travels fast. I didn't think you guys in Administration were that plugged in to Homicide."

"Oh, yeah, we know everything," Aldo assured me. Then he realized what he'd said. "I mean, not everything. Sometimes it's very hard to get information about certain things."

Probably the very information I'd called him for. "How about some pictures? Are those hard to come by?"

"That depends, Ronnie. What kind of pictures are you talking about?"

"Crime-scene photos. How's your access to something like that?"

"Uh."

"Payton Murphy. In the tub with a radio. I'd love to sneak a peek, Aldo. Any way you can arrange it?"

"Never!"

"Don't say never, Aldo."

"It's an open homicide, Ronnie. Aren't you still a suspect?"

"Well . . . they released me. I bet there's some way you could swing it. How about if I buy you lunch and we talk about it?"

"Lunch?"

The eagerness in his voice made me wince. And it pushed my guilt up another level. Aldo was so easy. "Right, Aldo. Lunch. I'm sure if we put our heads together and think, we can come up with something."

CHAPTER

8

WITH TWO HOURS TO kill before lunch I put in a call to Frankie Zola. The guy who answered told me Frankie was still out of town, but I left a message saying it was urgent I talk to him. That was just in case he knew anything about my Charlotte Murphy impostor.

Then I drove over to the Main Library, waded past the homeless on the front steps, and looked up *Payton Murphy*.

I sort of hopscotched through the microfilm. Most of the stuff about him was political. He championed legislature to save the coast, the whales, the farmers, and business profits from state taxes. Somehow he'd managed to be what every politician aspires to: all things to all people. According to the papers, everybody loved him.

I flipped back to last year and found a subdued, respectful piece about Charlotte Murphy's death in a Lake Tahoe boating accident and a reference without elaboration that it was the second time water had brought tragedy into the Senator's life. The article said Charlotte had been his second wife—the first one had died ten years earlier—and that she was thirty-three years old. Her picture didn't even come close to resembling the woman who'd hired me. The real Mrs. Murphy looked like Ivana Trump's dark cousin and the woman who'd hired me was more the Audrey Hepburn type.

As to the rest, all the articles were the same: praise and more praise for the Senator. Beyond the political, he was a quiet but effective man, a family man, an earnest and fit man who, until suffering a heart attack last year, had kept fit by jogging.

A couple of articles made reference to the fact that Murphy had a grandson who had suffered brain damage when he almost drowned in a swimming-pool accident, but they didn't even mention his name or when the accident had taken place. There was nothing about anybody else in his family. Whatever else Payton Murphy was, he was very careful about the press and his family.

I sat back and thought as the machine rewound the microfilm back onto its spool. Who would want Payton Murphy dead? According to the newspaper reports, nobody. Payton Murphy was Mr. Nice Guy.

But that was his public persona. Maybe on a personal level he wasn't so nice. Maybe the Charlotte Murphy impersonator was an ex-lover of his, someone he'd jilted, someone he'd done something awful to. But why drag me into it? Was that part personal? Or was I just a means to an end?

I spent the rest of the morning checking out the social pages looking for some mention of Murphy and who he might have dated. I ran across four blurbs and two pictures of Myra and seven of my Aunt Emily, but no Payton Murphy. No pictures of the fake Charlotte Murphy either.

I finally gave up and dropped down to the pay phones on the first floor. There was no answer at Blackie's, but Marcus at the Quarter Moon Saloon said he'd been by and left a message for me.

"He said to tell you he's going into personal politics," Marcus said. "That mean anything to you?"

Blackie was checking into Payton Murphy's personal life. Good. I hoped he'd have have better luck than I had.

By the time I walked into Big Morton's Chili Café, I was in a pretty sour mood. Not Aldo, though. He acted like a teen at the prom.

"This is a great place, Ronnie. I'm glad you suggested it. How'd you get reservations on such short notice?"

"I did their alarm system. They're grateful."

I didn't tell him I'd bartered my fee so the meal wouldn't cost me anything. I was still buying—it just wasn't with the usual currency. Besides, if Aldo knew, he'd probably arrest me or turn me in to the I.R.S.

The place was a little too social and trendy for

my taste, but I figured I could keep my eyes open for the alias Mrs. Murphy and hard-sell Aldo into giving me access to the photos at the same time.

We sat down, Aldo in his crisply starched blue jumpsuit setting his neat-as-a-pin backpack on the extra chair, and me, feeling both eager and guilty at the same time. *I* know I'll never go on a real date with Aldo, but I don't think *he's* realized it yet.

"How have you been, Ronnie?"

I smiled. He'd just handed me the perfect opening. "Really great—until Tuesday night," I said. "The D.A. thinks I'm guilty and they're trying to put a case together. They're just waiting for their witness to get better so he can talk."

"He should clear you then, shouldn't he?" Aldo was fishing. That made me uneasy. His allegiance to me from our high school days could only be stretched so far.

"Of course," I said, forcing a heartiness into my voice that I didn't quite feel. "But I don't know how long that's going to take and I'd kind of like to clear things up so I can get on with my life, you know?"

A waiter glided up and dumped a couple of bowls of chili, plates of salad, and sourdough on our table. That's what makes the place so trendy —it's a one-dish restaurant. Nobody ever has to order 'cause everybody gets the same thing. The "in-crowd" loves it.

"Something to drink?" our waiter asked.

"Anchor Steam," I said. "What about you, Aldo?"

"Milk. Skim milk."

I dove into the chili but Aldo had to polish his silverware first. When the waiter brought our drinks, Aldo had to make sure the rim of his glass didn't have any lipstick left over from the last person who'd used it. When he finally did take a bite of chili, he must have chewed it at least thirty times. Somebody's mother would have loved Aldo.

"So, Aldo, is there any point in the process where you can get your hands on these pictures?"

He squirmed and chewed, avoiding my eyes. When he finally swallowed, he nodded.

Yesss! Good old I-cannot-tell-a-lie Aldo.

"Hey, that's great, Aldo! We're halfway there."

"But, Ronnie, I don't know if this is right."

"I need to clear myself of a murder charge, Aldo. *Murder.* You know I didn't kill anybody, don't you?"

He dabbed at his thin lips with the napkin. "Yes."

The waiter swooped down, hauled away our dirty bowls, and set two plates of apple pie in front of us. With ice cream.

"So all I'm asking is a chance to prove it. That's all you'll be helping me to do, is prove my innocence. You know I'm innocent and I know it. All we've got left is to convince the D.A. so he won't press charges against me. He needs to go after the real killer. Isn't that how the justice system's supposed to work?''

"Actually . . ." Aldo drew himself up and I knew I'd gone too far. "The justice system would take you to trial and find you not guilty because you're not guilty. That's how the justice system would work. And I think you're being a little impatient, Ronnie. You should trust the system." He cut the tip off his wedge of apple pie and scooped up a bit of ice cream to go with it. "I think you'd be pleasantly surprised to see how it works."

While he was chewing his pie thirty times, I refocused my spiel.

"But the real killer could be getting away," I said. "He might even kill again. That's a possibility you need to consider. Every minute he's out, there's that possibility, Aldo. Can you live with that?"

Aldo's mouth was full, but his pale face registered alarm. He shook his head.

"That's why you've got to show me those pictures."

He swallowed. "Okay, Ronnie. I'll do it. But if anybody finds out—"

"Nobody's going to find out, Aldo. Trust me."

He dabbed at his skinny little lips again and put his refolded napkin down on the table. "I do, Ronnie. I trust you a lot." He reached over to his backpack and pulled out a folder. "Here."

"You brought them? Aldo! You're terrific!" I shoved my plate aside, set the folder on the table, and opened it.

The first picture was an eight-by-ten glossy of a naked man slumped in a marble tub with an expensive Sony radio balanced in the scummy water by his feet. Payton Murphy. The popular senator. His head was bent onto his chest so I couldn't see his face, which was for the better, I think.

At the foot of the tub on the left side of the frame was a small set of built-in shelves holding books and magazines. One of the shelves was empty, exposing an electrical outlet on the wall behind it. The cord from the radio was plugged in there.

I imagined the suave and gray-haired Payton Murphy I'd seen in the newspapers lolling in the tub, probably with his eyes closed, then . . . then what? Then somebody walked into the room and tossed the radio in the tub while he just sat there? Not likely.

I flipped quickly through the rest of the pictures, but the first one had told me all I needed to know: Payton Murphy hadn't struggled. He hadn't even tried to jump out of the tub when his killer walked in and crossed the room to the shelves. The killer had to be somebody he knew and trusted. A friend? A lover?

I handed back the folder. "Did you read the police report, Aldo?"

He squirmed. That meant yes.

"Did it say anything about who Murphy's been dating?"

"No."

"Whose fingerprints did they find on the radio? Anybody's?"

"Murphy's, his grandson's, the housekeeper's. Some others, but they were smudged."

Not mine, though. Thank God for that.

It wasn't until I was out on the street after Aldo had left that I realized he hadn't even tried to angle this into another lunch or dinner. *Maybe I'm in more trouble than I realize,* I thought, then shook my head and wandered off to find my car.

CHAPTER 9

I STOPPED IN AT Phoebe Wright's office just like the judge had told me to. Phoebe looked up from a ten-inch-thick file she'd been poring over.

Her desk and the floor around it was, as usual, littered with cardboard cartons filled with papers and more papers—only she called them "documents" and "exhibits."

She was wearing a gray suit today that matched the dark circles under her eyes, and her hair spiraled out around her face like blond electricity. When she saw me, she smiled.

"You get my message?" she asked.

"No. What did it say?"

She straightened her back and stretched. "It said Buddy Murphy was ready to talk and Scotch was going to interview him in an hour. That was at ten o'clock."

"Is Buddy the big retarded kid, the witness?"

"Right. But you can forget it. He crumbled."

"What do you mean?"

"He saw the police and flipped out again. They had to sedate him. The doctor says maybe they can try tomorrow. She's going to let them know how he is tomorrow afternoon."

"He must have seen something."

"Forget it, Ronnie. You're not going near him."

"Why else would he be upset when he sees the cops?"

She set her pencil down. "Tampering with a witness will *really* mess things up. Ronnie? Are you listening?"

"Sure. But are you hearing what I'm saying? Buddy Murphy *must* have seen something. He had to."

"You're *not* going to talk to him."

I thought a minute. "What if I see his doctor?"

"Why?"

"Just to talk. Find out how he's doing. See if she knows anything."

"I don't think you should go there without a witness."

"That's a great idea, Counselor. What are you doing this afternoon?"

Dr. Miranda Patel's office was in a low, flat building on California near Gough. Stickley Convalescent Building. The lobby was clean and bright, decorated with flowers and museum prints, and the woman staffing the front desk seemed cheerful. She sent us unsupervised down an antiseptic-smelling hall to a solid white door with DR. MIRANDA PATEL, DIRECTOR inscribed on it.

We found a receptionist inside who, after buzzing Dr. Patel, led us down a second, shorter hall lined with shelves full of thick medical books.

Dr. Patel rose from behind an elegant Victorian desk when her receptionist ushered us in. Her glistening black hair was tied into an elegant chignon. It gleamed the same shiny ebony as her eyes.

Her frame was compact and slender but she carried herself with authority. She smiled perfunctorily, showing very white teeth against brown skin, and came around the desk toward us.

"I can only give you fifteen minutes," she said, shaking our hands and leading us over to a small sitting area in the corner of the room. "Please sit down. Would you like some coffee? Perhaps some tea? No? Nothing, Mary. Thank you."

The receptionist quietly closed the door as Dr. Patel dropped gracefully into her armchair. Phoebe and I took the sofa.

Dr. Patel said, "Mr. Morgan didn't say he was sending more staff out."

Phoebe blanched. She started to say something but I cleared my throat loudly, smiled, and said, "We just have a few questions, Doctor."

Phoebe opened her mouth again. I kicked her ankle under the coffee table, but she was determined to blow it.

"The D.A.—" she began.

"—appreciates all the time you're giving," I

said. "This won't take long." I glanced sideways at Phoebe. She was shaking her head.

"I can't do this," she announced.

Dr. Patel cast a quick, questioning look in my direction before turning back to Phoebe. "I'm sorry?" she said.

Phoebe was staring at the floor like she was thinking things over. Then she exhaled, looked straight into Dr. Patel's sympathetic eyes, and said, "I'm not going to—"

I jumped to my feet, pulled her up with me, and sort of whisked her toward the door. "Go ahead," I said. "It's all right. You don't have to stay. Get some fresh air. I promise I won't be long. Phoebe hates hospitals," I explained over my shoulder as I shoved her into the hall.

I shut the door before she could protest, then prayed she'd leave us alone. I went back to the couch and offered Dr. Patel my sincerest and most apologetic smile.

"Something awful happened when she had her tonsils out," I lied. "She won't talk about it but every time she sees a doctor now, she gets hives."

Dr. Patel nodded gravely.

"So about Buddy Murphy . . . ?" I prompted.

"Buddy Murphy is still having a very difficult time. As I'm sure Mr. Morgan has told you, I'm afraid no one can see him now."

"As a matter of fact," I said, "I haven't seen Scotch Morgan today. Can you tell me what happened this morning?"

"Buddy regressed again. I told Mr. Morgan I'm

going to try again tomorrow, but I cannot make any promises.''

I leaned forward and tried to sound like a prosecutor—a nice one. "I know you've probably answered a lot of questions already, Doctor, probably the same questions I'm going to ask you, but please be patient. How long have you been treating Buddy?"

She joined her long tapered fingers and rested her hands on her lap. When she spoke, her voice was filled with affectionate pride.

"Buddy came to Stickley's day school three years ago. He was fifteen and had outgrown his former school. Sometimes when a mentally challenged person reaches puberty, he has difficulty understanding and coping with those changes. We've had enormous success guiding our patients through into full-functioning adulthood.

"We've been especially proud of Buddy because he's made so much progress and, until now, he was here on a nonresident basis. He was a star example that our retarded citizens need not be institutionalized."

"He lived with the Senator?"

"Yes. We kept Buddy here for a few short weeks at the beginning, but the Senator wanted Buddy at home. It's easier, of course, at the inception for the patient to live here, but Buddy excelled in spite of that additional obstacle."

"What happened to Buddy's parents?"

"Oftentimes the more educated and well-to-do a person is, the harder it is to accept a retarded offspring. I believe Buddy's mother, who was a single parent in addition to being very young at the time of his accident, didn't have the emotional wherewithal to deal with Buddy. Her father took over the parenting role and has been there for Buddy ever since."

"You're talking about the accident in the swimming pool?"

"Yes. As I explained to Mr. Morgan, when the brain suffers anoxia—lack of oxygen—it cannot survive unharmed. Buddy is clinically retarded, meaning he is retarded because of physiological reasons. As opposed to sociocultural ones. He was born with normal intelligence but was underwater and unconscious long enough to render him what we term mildly retarded. He has the mental and emotional capacities of a ten- or eleven-year-old. And as with anyone with limited mental powers, Buddy can grasp simple concepts and functions quite well as long as his environment is kept slow and uncomplicated. He thrives on routine, and the last few days have been far from routine."

"Has Buddy told you anything? About the murder, I mean?"

Dr. Patel sighed. "I think what you and Mr. Morgan fail to understand is that Buddy is very fragile right now. His entire world has been severely disrupted. He has suffered the loss of his primary caretaker. His grandfather, I think it is safe to say, was the person he cared for most. You must allow him the time he needs, the time any person needs, to grieve for his loved one."

"But why would seeing the police scare him so much? Why would that make him regress? It sounds to me like he must have witnessed something."

"Perhaps. But the simple fact that he is disturbed by the police isn't that unusual. He would naturally associate them with the horror of that night. He may or he may not have seen a murder committed. If he did, he may or may not have been or even now be aware of its significance. What Buddy knows is that his life has been altered, but he doesn't quite grasp, much less understand, why or how."

It was pretty clear she was sold on that explanation and wasn't going to tell me more, so I tried a new tack.

"How did Buddy and the Senator get along?"

"Buddy adored his grandfather."

"Didn't Buddy ever get mad at him?"

Dr. Patel smiled benignly as she shook her head. "Buddy is extremely sweet-natured."

"Things change, Dr. Patel. People change."

Her expression didn't waver, but her voice lost its warmth. "What are you implying?"

I shrugged. "Something could have altered their relationship. Do you know, for instance, if Senator Murphy's been seeing anybody since his wife died?"

She was obviously annoyed with the question and didn't bother to hide it. "I have no idea," she answered curtly. "And if you think Buddy capable of murder, then you're not a very good judge of character."

"I haven't met Buddy Murphy, Dr. Patel. And I'm not accusing anybody. I'm just trying to get to the bottom of this. After all, the whole thing could even have been an accident."

She seemed happy with that possibility, so I said, "Was there anything new or different about Buddy lately? Any change in behavior? Anything odd about how he went through his daily routine?"

She watched me, still wary.

"Please, Doctor."

She started to shake her head, then paused. "It's not significant," she said. "And it's not new behavior."

"Tell me."

She pressed her lips together.

"Please."

"It's perfectly normal," she began. "And it's never a cause for concern. It's merely a stage some children go through."

"What?"

"Buddy has invented an imaginary friend. He's made someone up, a best friend, someone to share his thoughts with."

She smiled indulgently at my puzzled expression and went on, warming to the role of lecturer. "It's a coping mechanism. Children do this sometimes when they're not getting enough attention from outside sources. And of course Buddy has always been very creative. Imaginary friends are often an outgrowth of creativity.

"This phenomenon usually occurs in four- or five-year-olds, but science doesn't know everything about the retarded mind. Most children outgrow their imagined friends. Some have more than one, and some of our mentally challenged children keep them their whole lives. As I said, it's not at all unusual or remarkable."

"What has Buddy told you about this friend?"

"He says she's beautiful and smart and she tells him he's smart too. That's one of Buddy's secret wishes, to be as smart as everyone else."

I thought a minute. His friend didn't sound so fabulous to me. "Why can't she be real?"

"To begin with, Buddy told me she took him to the zoo and to the cinema and to a video arcade all in one afternoon. It's obvious these are fantasies, activities Buddy never has the opportunity to indulge in but would like to.

"Secondly, she's too good to be true. Buddy says she's beautiful, cares for him deeply, and never refuses him anything. Spend an hour with Buddy and, charming though he is, see how impossible it is not to say no. He's good-natured and he's creative. That's why he's constantly testing those around him."

"But—"

"Another reason I know his friend is invented is because Buddy's schedule is very full. I suppose he could take an afternoon or evening off without me or his grandfather knowing about it but it would be hard."

"Did you mention this imaginary friend to Scotch Morgan?"

"He didn't seem to think it significant."

But I did. Maybe Buddy Murphy had gone off the deep end. The murderers in all those horror movies always have secret friends, voices they hear that tell them to kill. Maybe Payton Murphy tells him no one time too many, the nerves snap, and voices tell him to toss the radio into the tub.

But who tipped the police? And who was the woman calling herself Charlotte Murphy?

I stepped into the sunshine outside Dr. Patel's office and headed for my car.

Phoebe was standing next to it, arms crossed, brows furrowed, tapping her foot. Her frizzy blond hair stood on end and she looked un-happy.

"Are you crazy?" she demanded when I reached her. "I could get disbarred for this."

"For what?"

"You know for what."

"I didn't go in there with the intent to scam her, Phoebe. And neither did you. She made the mistake, and I just went along with it. Besides, do you think she would have been forthcoming if she knew I was the accused?"

"Of course not." Phoebe pushed her tangled curls off her forehead and narrowed her eyes. "Listen, Ronnie. I admire your ability to get information but I don't think you should investigate anymore."

"But—"

"I mean it. You hired me to be your lawyer and I'm giving you lawyerly advice. Don't hand them a gift-wrapped, bow-tied guilty plea. That's what you'll be doing if you keep this up. You look pretty bad already."

"How am I going to look worse? I get invited to test somebody's burglar alarm by a woman who died a year ago, and just by coincidence there's a freshly dead body upstairs, and just by coincidence the police get tipped the instant I set foot in the house. Now, you tell me, how are things going to look any worse?"

"All I'm saying is that if the police catch you investigating like this, they'll put you in jail and keep you there until you go to trial. Is that what you want?"

I opened the car door and got in.

When Phoebe was settled in beside me, she said, "Well?"

"Well, what?"

"Did Dr. Patel tell you anything worth losing your license over?"

I shrugged. "The retarded guy's got an imaginary friend."

Phoebe looked unimpressed.

"That means he's not real plugged in to reality," I explained.

"Are you suggesting he killed Payton Murphy?"

"Why not? I'm thinking he could be hearing voices, you know, voices that say, 'Kill your grandfather.' "

Phoebe stared. She looked as uncomfortable as I felt accusing a retarded boy of murdering his own flesh-and-blood.

"Of course that doesn't explain Charlotte Murphy or the phone tip," I said quickly. "Maybe his secret friend is my Charlotte Murphy."

Phoebe frowned and shook her head. Her electrified curls bounced. "Not a good angle."

"Why not?"

"Scotch Morgan's been saying all along that you made her up. If I know him, he'll take this and somehow wrangle it into an admission that you killed Payton Murphy."

"Great." I put the car in gear and drove.

When I pulled up outside Phoebe's office on outer Post near Japantown, she paused with her hand on the lever that would open the door.

"Where are you going from here?"

I glanced at the clock on the dash. Four-thirty. The sign outside the Trap and Saddle said they closed at five. I smiled.

"I'm going to see a woman about a scarf," I said.

Phoebe pulled her briefcase out with her, then leaned back inside the car.

"Just don't get caught," she said, not smiling, then shut the door and headed into her building.

CHAPTER

10

AT 5:05 KATHERINE, the salesclerk from the Trap and Saddle, zipped out the door without a backward glance and headed straight for the bus stop outside the Sutter-Stockton Garage.

I queued up a few feet behind her, near the very spot where Dashiell Hammett had dumped the body of Sam Spade's partner, Miles Archer.

When the 30 Stockton bus came and Katherine got on, she was lucky enough to get a seat. I wasn't. I got shuffled down the bus's narrow center aisle along with the rest of the riders and grabbed an overhead metal hand bar just as the bus lurched forward. The whole group stiffened, all of us trying to keep our balance as the electric bus whirred and plunged into the blackness of the Stockton Street tunnel.

When we came out at the other end, we were in Chinatown. I searched the bobbing heads in front of me for Katherine's. She was still there, on the left, two rows up from the back door. Her head was bowed. Maybe she was reading.

I squeezed past a couple of older Chinese women clutching pink plastic bags full of mysterious vegetables and odd-smelling parcels, past a trio of chattering secretary types and two men in suits. By the time we reached Sacramento Street, I was standing next to Katherine. She was paging through a thick, glossy magazine, oblivious to everybody around her.

"Hi, Katherine," I said.

She looked up, startled, but with an expectant half smile on her bright red lips. When she saw me, though, the smile vanished. Her face drained of color. She blinked, like a frightened animal, then her eyes darted to the front door like she was considering making a run for it. Cedric must have really done a number on her.

"I guess you remember me?" I asked pleasantly.

"What do you want?" She sounded scared. A few passengers turned in our direction, interest percolating under their usually stony commuter faces. Katherine's open magazine lay forgotten on her lap.

"I just need to ask you a few questions."

She shook her head. "I don't know anything."

By now the whole passenger load was tuned in. The bus lurched to a stop. Nobody got off and about ten more people were jamming themselves on up front.

"I need to know about those scarves."

She turned away, shaking her head again and staring out the window toward the group on the sidewalk waiting to board.

"The Siven scarves," I said. "Katherine?"

At the sound of her name, she pulled her eyes off the group on the sidewalk and looked up at me.

"I—I can't talk to you. Please leave me alone." She closed her magazine and stared out the window again, pretending I wasn't there.

"Katherine, please, this involves murder. I need your help."

"Sorry."

Something outside caught my eye. Something familiar, a flash of color. I glanced at the group waiting to board out on the sidewalk and gasped. There, Siven scarf draped tastefully around her neck and staring straight at me, was my Charlotte Murphy impostor. Our eyes locked.

I willed her not to move. I prayed that she was real. Keeping my eyes on hers, I started making my way toward the back door. As soon as I reached the halfway point, she turned and ran.

I shoved my way through the remaining mass of bodies and reached the door just as the bus lurched into motion.

"Back door!" I shouted. "Back door!"

The bus hummed blithely down one block, then another while I pounded my fist against the door and kept on shouting.

It finally stopped three blocks later. I dove out and hit the sidewalk running. But when I got to where Charlotte Murphy had been, she was gone.

CHAPTER 11

I DON'T KNOW WHY I went back to Payton Murphy's house at dusk, but I did. I'd run up and down Stockton Street until I was nearly blind. I'd thought about going to Philly Post, then decided there was really nothing he would do and basically nothing he *could* do.

So I checked my answering machine for messages and found out Frankie Zola had phoned saying he hadn't given my name to anybody since last year and, if I had the time, could I maybe wire a warehouse he was buying next month? So much for that lead.

I drove around feeling bummed until I found myself in Presidio Heights again. I pulled the Toyota up across the street and just sat there in the dark, staring at the house and trying to figure out why my mystery woman would want to kill Murphy and frame me.

I didn't know her. I'd never seen her before in my life. She had to have been aware of that to sit through lunch with me and ask me to break into Murphy's house. Maybe I was just a luckless pawn. Maybe the murderer had just used me because I was a convenient way to deflect attention away from her.

Then again the whole mess could be just a series of awful coincidences. I could have flubbed her name—maybe she'd said Murray, not Murphy. I could have gotten the wrong address, and Payton Murphy could have accidentally dropped the radio into his bath at the very instant a neighbor saw me break in. Weirder stuff has happened.

The moon was rising from behind the hill that was Pacific Heights, casting a nice bright light over everything. I was debating whether I should try breaking into Payton Murphy's house again or just go home and get some rest when a figure wandered out from Murphy's backyard and made its way to the front door of the house.

I watched the shadow, my heart in my throat. He was male, heavyset, with a meandering, shuffling gait that made me think he could be drunk or drugged. He wandered up to the door and light sprung around him like an aura. Then his back shifted and I saw he held a flashlight in his hand. He shone the light on the front door and fumbled with the knob for a while, then gave up.

He rang the bell, waited, then shut off the flashlight as he turned away and shuffled down the front walk, head down, the picture of dejection.

As he came down the sidewalk toward my car, I

glimpsed his slack features and realized who he was. I rolled my window down and called out softly. "Buddy?"

He stopped under the amber glow of the street-lamp and looked around, mouth open, confusion and fear clouding his gentle face. I tried to picture this puzzled, harmless-looking person as a cold-blooded killer. Dr. Patel was right; he didn't fit the part.

"Over here," I said, opening the car door and stepping out into the light.

As I started toward him, he raised his hand in a sloppy wave, then froze, the beginning of what could have been a huge smile arrested on his face. I got a quick look at his dilated pupils before he blinked and averted his eyes.

"You're Buddy Murphy, aren't you?"

He nodded, keeping his head down, eyes on the pavement like he'd been caught doing something bad. Or maybe he was just bashful.

He wore loose-fitting chinos, high-tops, and a flannel shirt under a plaid jacket. I couldn't see his eyes, or much of his face for that matter, until he raised his head and held my gaze with an earnestly puzzled expression on his childlike face.

"I thought you was somebody else," he muttered in a voice so soft I had to lean forward to hear. "I thought you was a friend of mine."

"I'd like to be your friend," I said.

His smile was tentative, uncertain, then suddenly broad and full of enthusiasm. "Yeah?"

I extended my hand. "My name's Ronnie."

His jaw fell, and his head jerked back like somebody had punched him in the nose. He studied my face, then shook his head emphatically. "You're not Ronnie," he said. "I know Ronnie."

I tried to make sense out of what he was saying, and finally it struck me. "Sometimes two people have the same name, Buddy."

I searched my mind for a famous example he might have heard of but I drew a blank. He frowned, keeping his dilated eyes on me, waiting. You could almost touch the frustration and confusion behind his drugged expression.

"You're not Ronnie," he repeated with growing petulance. "I *know* Ronnie."

I was losing him. I needed to come up with something that made sense to him. "How about Ronnie Vee? You want to call me Ronnie Vee?"

"Ronnie Vee." He smiled, then offered me his hand. "I'm Buddy, Ronnie Vee. I'm pleased to meet you, Ronnie Vee."

His grip was crushing. He pumped our hands up and down in an exaggerated handshake that lasted almost a whole minute. "Please to meet you, Ronnie Vee."

I pulled my hand out of his gently.

"I'm pleased to meet you, too, Buddy. Can we be friends?"

"Uh-huh. I'd like that. But you can't be my best friend. I got a best friend already."

"That's okay. We'll just be regular friends."

I was starting to feel pretty obvious standing out

in the street, so I gestured toward the car. "Let's stand over here and talk, okay?"

He ambled over with me, feet shuffling like a giant panda's, then stood on the sidewalk next to the passenger side of the car with his big arms hanging down limp in front of him, watching me with a slow eagerness.

"What are you doing here, Buddy?" I asked. "I thought you were at the hospital."

"I don't like the hospital. They won't give me any candy. See that house?" He pointed to the brown shingle. "I live in that house. And I got candy in my room. In a box. It's a real pretty tin box with a picture of a eagle on it. It's blue and gold except for the eagle. He's black and white and brown. And there's candy inside of it. Candy and special things. Lots of candy." He turned toward the house and gestured broadly. "But Daddy Murphy won't open the door, and I forgot my key. He locked the door. Do you have a key?"

I hesitated. His childlike eyes pleaded.

"Sort of," I said. "Let me move my car first. You want to ride with me?"

Wariness crept over his face. "I'm not supposed to ride in strangers' cars," he said.

"We're not strangers, Buddy. I know your name and you know mine. Strangers don't know each other's names, do they?"

He grinned. "Yeah!" He laughed as he reached for the passenger-side door and dove into the Toyota.

His bulk filled the small bucket seat. As the engine turned over, I could hear him breathe. It was a labored, raspy sound, like somebody with asthma. I didn't want him collapsing in front of me. The cops would probably arrest me for the asthma attack then.

"Do you have asthma, Buddy?" I asked.

"What's that?"

"It's an illness. Makes it hard for you to breathe."

"No. I had the measles once. And the chicken pox. But I never got the asthma," he said. He looked around the car. "I like riding in cars. I'm gonna drive one someday. Pop said I might. Some day."

"Pop?" Dr. Patel had said he didn't have a father. "Who's Pop?"

"Daddy Murphy. I call him Pop sometimes."

I'd started having second thoughts about breaking into Payton Murphy's house again, so I pulled over at the end of the block and said, "How about if we just go somewhere and eat? Are you hungry, Buddy?"

"Yeah! I'm always hungry. I like French fries a lot. And milk shakes. Will you buy me a milk shake, Ronnie Vee?"

I drove down to Lombard Street and pulled up in front of a neon-lit hamburger joint. "Let's try this place," I said. "Have you ever been to Clown Alley?"

Buddy Murphy swallowed his milk shake in about a minute and a half. When he finished it, he slammed the empty waxed cup down on the table with relish and, grinning broadly, asked, "Can I have another one?"

I looked into his eager, childlike face. His features were conventionally attractive—strong chin, broad forehead, thick curly brown hair—but his facial muscles sagged and there was a dullness in his eyes that took the luster from his looks.

He didn't seem as sluggish now as he had back at the house. His pupils were still dilated, though. Maybe he needed something solid in his stomach. "Eat your French fries first, okay?"

He nodded and reached for the steaming packet I'd set between us.

"Listen, Buddy. We've got to talk."

"Uh-huh." He shoved a handful of fries into his mouth. When he chewed, he kept his mouth open, so I tried to focus on just his eyes.

"Something happened at your house the other night," I began.

He stopped chewing and averted his eyes.

"Buddy?"

He looked up, and his expression had changed into something unmistakable—terror. He glanced around the small restaurant, dropped the bag of fries on the table, and hugged his arms tightly across his chest.

"It's okay, Buddy. Nothing's going to happen to you now. You're safe now. I just need to know what happened the other night. Can you tell me about it?"

He started shaking his head, slowly at first, then in quick, violent sweeps. He thrust his right arm out and swept the table clean, hurling French fries, napkins, and cups across the room.

"NO!" he shouted, rising from his chair like King Kong about to topple Manhattan. Chewed-up French fries spewed out of his mouth. "NO-NO-NO-NO!"

The two guys behind the counter stopped their conversation and stared. A homeless guy camped out over a cup of coffee in the corner looked alarmed but didn't dare move.

"Buddy," I said. One minute he was standing, his chair toppled at an odd angle on the floor behind him, and the next he was headed for the door. The guys at the register sort of ducked behind the counter as he stormed past them.

"Wait, Buddy. Wait!"

I ran out the door after him. "Come on, Buddy. I won't make you talk about that, okay? I promise. We'll talk about something else."

He stopped about ten feet from the car and clumsily wheeled to face me. His anguish tore at my heart.

"I wanta go home," he sobbed.

When I pulled onto West Pacific Avenue, there was a car parked across the street in front of Payton Murphy's house.

"Tell you what, Buddy. We're going to have to drive by your house without stopping first, okay?"

"Why?"

"See that car over there in front of your house?"

"Yeah."

"It looks like the guy inside it is looking at your house, doesn't it?"

"Uh-huh."

"Okay. When we drive by, I want you to look at your house too. Try to see what he's looking at, okay?"

"Okay."

He hunched forward and put his face up to the side window. When we drove by the parked car, all the person could see was the back of Buddy's head. But I got a good look at him and he got a good look at me. I'd never seen him before in my life. But his car was unmistakable. Unmarked police. Great.

"I want ta go home," Buddy whined when we reached the end of the block. "I want ta go *home.*"

I turned the corner and kept going. "That guy," I said, "that guy parked in front of your house wants to take you back to the hospital."

"NO!" Buddy shouted. "I don't want to go back! I won't! I want to go *HOME*!"

He wouldn't shut up, so I ended up driving up through the Presidio to the back of his house with every intention of dropping him off in his backyard. I knew the cop in the car would see him the instant he wandered around the front.

He'd take him to the hospital, but I was starting to think the hospital was where Buddy needed to be for now. It was pretty clear I wasn't going to get anything out of him while he was in the shape he was in now. It was his own backyard, after all.

But when I got there, I couldn't do it.

Instead of slowing down, I shoved my foot onto the gas. We sped by his yard.

"I'll buy you candy, Buddy," I said. "I'll buy you all the candy you want, okay? Just don't make me take you home."

CHAPTER
12

BLACKIE WAS HOME and awake, taking in a boxing match on cable the usual way he liked to watch them—with the sound off and soft, incongruent jazz playing in the background.

He always looks younger when he smiles, and that's just what he did when he opened the door to his tiny Bernal Heights shack and found us on his doorstep.

"What the hell, Ventana? Keepin' out of stir?" He chuckled and swung the door open for us to pass. "Who's your buddy?"

Buddy Murphy grinned. "How'd you know my name? Did Ronnie Vee tell you my name?"

Blackie stared at him hard for a second, then offered Buddy his hand.

"Buddy, huh? Well, Buddy, my name's Blackie." Blackie shook Buddy's hand and slapped him on the back. "What have you got in that bag there, Buddy?"

"Candy. Ronnie Vee bought me candy."

"That's great. Why don't you sit on the couch over there and get to work on it, Buddy? Me and Ronnie are going to have a talk in the kitchen."

I followed Blackie into his trashed-up kitchen. He shut the door, then pegged me with his steely blue eyes. "That's the missing kid," he growled.

"Missing? Who says he's missing?"

"They broke into the third round to show his picture, Ventana. Said he's a homicide witness. Where'd you get him?"

"He was wandering around his front yard. It's not that big a deal."

"Fuck, Ventana. It *is* a big deal. The cops call it kidnapping. It's a felony."

"He saw something, Blackie. I know he did."

"Won't matter what he saw if they nail you for kidnapping. Philly Post'll be the first to testify against you. You got to get rid of this guy. He's a liability, doll. You got rocks in your head if you don't see that."

"But—"

"Lose him, Ventana," he said with unmistakable finality. "He's not staying here."

"But they drugged him, Blackie. How's he going to remember anything if they stuff him full of drugs? Did you see his pupils? They were the size of basketballs when I found him. He's gotten better just in the last hour. I think whatever they gave him is wearing off and we can ask him about what happened pretty soon. At the very least we can find out if Murphy was dating anybody. Just give me a couple of hours."

Blackie yanked a pack of cigarettes from his pants pocket.

"Two hours," I said, watching him pull one out and light it.

He blew smoke into the air over our heads and stifled a belch. "Fuck, Ventana."

By ten-thirty Buddy had bonded with Blackie like he was his long-lost favorite uncle. And I could see why. Blackie was wonderful. He treated Buddy like he would any big, luggy kid, gruff but kind and respectful. Buddy lapped it up.

I finally managed to wrangle Blackie back into the kitchen for a minute while Buddy played with the torn-apart motorcycle engine Blackie's son, Joey, had brought over and forgotten in the corner of the living room about ten years ago.

"I think we can ask him now," I said.

Blackie's expression turned sour. "Have a heart, doll. The kid's havin' a good time."

"I'm risking felony charges, remember? We've got to ask him."

Blackie opened the fridge and pulled out an Anchor Steam. "You want one?"

"Sure." I took it, opened it, and drank a long swallow. "Okay. *I'll* ask him. But if he gets hysterical again, you talk him down, okay?"

Blackie gave me a disgusted look and shook his head. "Fuck, Ventana. I never thought you were this heartless."

"Heartless? It'll help him to talk about it. Isn't that what they always say? Don't bury your grief?

Besides, he saw something. I know he did, Blackie.''

When we marched into the living room, Buddy held up two engine parts he'd tied together with a stray wire and grinned with pride at his accomplishment.

"I'm puttin' it together," he said. "I'm makin' it back into a motorcycle so I can ride it.''

I sat down on the floor beside him and asked him if he wanted another Coke, but he still had some left. "About that night," I began.

He went quiet and seemed to withdraw into himself. The parts in his hands just hung there, then he dropped his hands, still holding the parts, onto his lap. Grease stained his chinos. At least he wasn't screaming and violent like he'd been at Clown Alley. Not yet.

"Buddy," I said softly. "Did your grandfather have a girlfriend? Was he dating anybody?''

He thought a minute, fingers toying idly with the wire, then shook his head. "Nope.''

"Nobody?''

"Huh-uh.''

Maybe he didn't know. Maybe his grandfather wouldn't tell him something like that.

But behind me Blackie said, "He's playing straight with you, doll. I checked it out. Nobody in the past year.''

I tried again. "About the other night, Buddy.''

He looked up. His guileless face sagged with grief.

"Blackie and I need to know what happened, Buddy. Do you think you can talk about it now?"

He turned away and shuddered. Blackie leaned forward into my line of vision and caught my eye.

"Hey, doll." He shook his head imperceptibly. A warning. I frowned back at him and moved in closer.

"Buddy. We want to help you but we can't unless you tell us what you saw that night."

"Help?" Buddy's voice was a tiny whisper.

"Yes. Somebody hurt your grandfather and—"

He inhaled sharply. Still staring at the floor, he whimpered. "They told me Daddy Payton's dead. At the hospital they said he's dead. That's what Dr. Patel said. She woke me up and told me. Dead-dead-DEAD!" Then in that tiny, breathless whisper: "It's not true, Ronnie Vee, is it?"

I nodded. "I'm sorry, Buddy."

"They told us about 'dead.' At school. 'Dead' is when you don't come back. God takes your soul to heaven and you don't come back. If Daddy Payton is dead, does that mean he's never coming back?"

Buddy started swaying, rocking silently back and forth, arms drawn tight around his body, hugging himself, comforting himself. The engine parts lay forgotten on the floor as he seemed to withdraw even farther.

"Buddy? *Buddy?*"

He didn't seem to hear. He just kept rocking and swaying. Blackie cleared his throat.

Finally, after a minute that seemed to last forever, a big tear rolled out the corner of Buddy's left eye. Then the right one followed and he let out a big, heart-wrenching sob. I reached over and patted his shoulder.

"I'm sorry, Buddy. I'm sorry he's gone."

"He *liked* the radio," Buddy mumbled. "He liked it a lot. An—an—and it was dark and he knows I'm scared a the dark."

"Sure you are, Buddy," I said, patting his quivering shoulder as he sobbed some more. I let him cry for a while, then said, "Did you see anybody in your house that night?"

He covered his ears and shook his head, hunkered down on the floor, swaying and sobbing, a long string of saliva hanging from the corner of his contorted mouth.

I didn't have the heart to press him anymore. Blackie probably would have slugged me if I had, so we cleared off a cot in the back bedroom and tucked him in, then left the hall light on and the door open for him and went back to the living room.

Blackie didn't say a word until we'd both finished our Anchor Steams. Then he went into the kitchen and came back with a pair of fresh ones.

"Kid's busted up," he said, settling on the threadbare couch and taking a long swig from the bottle.

I remembered how the pain had never seemed to stop when my own parents died. I thought of how much it still hurts, even now, almost twenty years later. Every time I realize that nothing,

nothing in the world will ever fill that huge, empty part of my life, I'm fourteen all over again, sobbing my eyes out, crying alone in the dark.

I looked up. Blackie was watching me. No pity, no sympathy in his eyes, just a careful and respectful distance, like he'd read my mind. I raised the bottle, took a slow, cold drink, and pushed my sad thoughts aside.

"What do you think, Blackie? Does it sound like he saw something?"

Blackie reached for a smoke and lit it, blowing a blue-gray puff into the air over his grizzled head.

"You know what I think? I think if he saw anything he'd just curl up in a ball and cry, Ventana."

A gentle sob filtered out from the back bedroom. I felt crummy—not just for trying to get information from a grief-stricken retarded boy but for Buddy's loss, for the whole unfairness of it.

"What's gonna happen to him?" Blackie asked after a while.

"I don't know."

Blackie frowned. "He's a good kid," he said, like maybe that might protect Buddy from getting hurt anymore.

I thought about the murderer who had taken Payton Murphy's life, the person who had set me up to take the blame, the person who was still roaming free somewhere ready, maybe, to do more harm. And I wondered if Buddy was safe.

CHAPTER
13

WE LET BUDDY sleep until noon the next day. He'd awakened in a somber but calmer mood with his eyes clear of any trace of yesterday's sedatives. And some of the grief and anger had been sobbed out of him, too, I guess, because he seemed lighter in spirit than he had last night.

We fed him three take-out MacDonald's fish sandwiches for breakfast which he ate sitting on Blackie's tattered, lumpy couch.

Then we listened in surprise as he announced he had to go to work.

"Blackie says it's Saturday," he said. "I always work Saturday. And Monday and Wednesday. I can take the bus. Do you know where I can catch the bus, Ronnie Vee? I have to catch the fifteen Sacramento. That bus takes me right to the front door."

Blackie and I exchanged looks.

"Okay," I said reluctantly. "We can take you if that's what you want, Buddy. But you should know that if you go to work, they'll come and take you back to the hospital.''

''No!'' He shook his head. ''I don't want to go to the hospital.''

I shrugged sympathetically. ''That's the way it is, Buddy.''

''But I *got* to go to work.''

''She's being straight with you, sport. You show up and they're going to call the hospital.''

Buddy's face crumpled. ''I don't want to go to the hospital,'' he sobbed. ''I don't like it there.''

He fixed red-rimmed eyes on me. ''I want to stay with Blackie. Can I live with you, Blackie?''

''You can visit, pal, but you can't stay.''

Buddy nodded soberly. ''I want to go home, then. I don't want to go to the hospital. I *won't* go to the hospital. They don't have candy there.'' He rose, pulled a peppermint stick out of his sack of candy, and said, ''I gotta go to work.''

''Looks like you're going to have to skip work today, Buddy, if you don't want to go back to the hospital.''

''But Joe's gonna fire me if I miss a day.''

''They'll fire you if you don't have a note from the hospital,'' I lied, feeling crummy about it.

He hung his head. ''I won't go to that hospital, Ronnie Vee. I want to go home. I want to see Daddy Payton.''

''You can't,'' I said gently. ''Remember? He's gone.''

Buddy thought a moment, then looked up at me and smiled. ''Mama won't make me go back. I want to go see Mama.''

CHAPTER

14

FOR THE PURPOSE of disguise Blackie gave Buddy a blue baseball cap to wear. Buddy was ecstatic.

"Can I keep this hat?" he asked about a million times between calling out directions that led us along the roundabout bus route that would lead us to his mother's house.

"When was the last time you saw your mom?" I asked as we came up behind a bus.

He'd already told us her name was Sondra and that she was dark-haired and about my size—she could easily be the woman who had called herself Charlotte Murphy.

"There's the bus!" Buddy cried excitedly. "That's the bus, Blackie. Just follow that bus."

"When did you see her, Buddy?" I asked again.

Buddy grinned and adjusted his cap, keeping his eye on the graffiti-marred bus in front of us. "Last week."

"Where?"

"My house. She was s'pposed to have dinner

but she yelled at Daddy Payton an' so he said she couldn't stay." He spotted a playground filled with children and his eyes lingered on them as we drove by.

"Buddy?"

He swung his big head around. "That's a nice swing," he said.

"What did they fight about?"

He frowned, concentrating, trying to remember. "Mama asked Daddy Payton for some money. But he wouldn't give it to her 'cause he says she's sick. He said it would be just like throwing money out a window."

The bus turned right, and we fell in behind it.

"I told Mama she could have my money an' that made her smile. I think she likes me. But when she counted it, she said it wasn't enough. She wanted Daddy Payton to give her some more."

"Did she say what she wanted the money for?"

"I'm not supposed to tell. She made me promise not to tell."

"Was it for medicine?" I asked.

He looked surprised and started to nod, then checked himself. "I'm not supposed to tell," he said. "She won't like me if I tell. She said people who can't keep secrets are stupid. I don't want to be stupid."

Buddy finally told us to stop near a dilapidated Victorian on Capp in the heart of the Mission. A couple of winos hung out on the front stoop. Watchdogs.

"How do you know this place?" I asked. "Did your mom bring you here?"

"Uh-huh. It was messy. A bunch of people were sleeping on the floor, and I had to be quiet."

"You're sure this is the place?" I asked. It was a world apart from Payton Murphy's Presidio Heights house.

Buddy glanced at the bus stop behind us, then back at the building. "Yeah, Ronnie Vee. My mama lives right there."

Sliding across the backseat, he reached for the door handle.

"Hold on, sport," Blackie said.

Buddy froze. "Aren't we gonna visit Mama?"

The winos had spotted us. They were sitting up a little straighter now and the hand of the scrungiest one had disappeared into his pocket. Since I doubted anybody would trust him with a gun, he was probably pressing the button on whatever remote alarm he'd been given by the dealer upstairs.

I glanced at Buddy's eager face and realized I couldn't confront his mother and accuse her of murder with him standing right there.

Blackie must have read my mind because he caught Buddy's eye and said, "Can't do it now, sport. No time."

Buddy hesitated, then released his grip on the door handle and sat back in his seat. "Do you think those people are still sleeping in there, Blackie? I don't like having to be quiet. An' the place smelled kinda funny."

Blackie's jaw tightened as he threw the car into gear and we headed down the street.

"You were upstairs, huh?" Blackie asked.

Buddy nodded. "It's messy in there. Real messy. Messier even than your house, Blackie. I bet that's why Mama don't want Daddy Payton to know I was there. I'm not supposed to tell. But it's wrong to lie. If Daddy Payton woulda asked me did I go where Mama lived, I woulda had to say yes. But Mama said if you love somebody, it's not wrong to lie if they ask you to, if they ask you to keep a secret. Mama asked me if I loved her and I said yes. But I'm glad Daddy Payton never asked me. I couldn't a lied to Daddy Payton."

Blackie turned onto Mission and headed north. Buddy scooted forward and folded his arms along the top of the front seat. "Where are we going now, Blackie?"

"Good question, sport." Blackie reached for a smoke and caught my eye. "Your call, doll."

I turned and looked into Buddy's eager face. "Blackie and I have got some work to do, Buddy. So while we're doing that, we need you to do us a favor. How about it?"

"Yeah! I'll do a favor for you and Blackie anytime."

"Good. Now, pay attention," I said. "I want you to practice saying . . ."

CHAPTER

15

MYRA OPENED THE door to her apartment and looked at Buddy. He was grinning at her from under the blue baseball cap and he performed just like I'd coached him to.

"Hi, Myra," he said.

Myra gaped, then looked past his shoulder at me.

"My God, Ronnie! It's the kidnapped boy."

"He's *not* kidnapped, Myra." I gave Buddy a nudge so he'd move into the living room.

"But—" She recoiled from Buddy as he passed by, her face filled with a perplexed kind of horror. "Why bring him here?"

I shut the door behind us and motioned for Buddy to sit on the couch. He ambled over and sat down, resting his hands on his knees as he gazed around the apartment with bright curiosity.

"Don't talk about Buddy like he doesn't understand," I said. "You understand what Myra's saying, don't you, Buddy?"

Buddy looked up, grinned, and nodded. "Uh-huh. Can I touch that bear?" He pointed to a stuffed calico-covered bear on a side table by the wall.

"That's an antique," Myra said quickly, turning to me. "Will he hurt it?"

I gestured toward Buddy. "Ask him."

"I won't hurt it, Myra. I promise. I just want to touch it."

"Well, okay. But it's over a hundred years old."

"A hundred! That's a lot of years," Buddy said. "I can't even count to a hundred."

Myra forced a smile at Buddy, then beckoned me into the corner of the room. Our backs were to Buddy as he rose and headed for the side table.

"Why did you bring him here?" Myra whispered.

"I need someplace safe for him."

She grimaced. "Doesn't Blackie usually do this sort of thing for you?"

"Blackie's too obvious. Besides, he's helping me in other ways." He'd dropped us off at my car and was probably already staking out Sondra Murphy's apartment.

"He's *not* staying here, Ronnie."

"Come on, Myra. You owe me."

She drew herself up. "For what?"

I started counting off on my fingers. "Two months running your tuxedo messages while you were in Amsterdam. Covering for you on your dog-walking service that time you sprained your ankle—"

"That was only a week and a half."

"Exposing that bigamist your mom wanted to marry. And going out on that double date with that bits-and-bytes Silicon Valley wonk last month. You *owe* me, Myra."

She glanced across the room to Buddy, who by now was totally absorbed smiling down at the stuffed bear in his lap and stroking it gently.

"All right," she said. "Just for today. But I've got some accounts I need to call on this afternoon."

"Call on, as in telephone?"

"I've got to visit them."

"It's Saturday, Myra." She was probably trying to squirrel out on me.

"They were too busy for me to call on them during the week."

"You're selling cellular phones. Why don't you just use the phone?"

"It doesn't work that way. Look, it'll just take me an hour, okay?" She checked her watch. "I'll be back by two."

I sighed. "Have you got any food?"

She nodded.

"Two o'clock," I said as she snatched up her briefcase and hurried out the door.

I glanced over at Buddy. He was sitting cross-legged now on the floor in front of the couch with Myra's stuffed bear propped up in front of him. He was muttering to himself and moving the bear's arms up and down, pretending that the bear was talking. Maybe he was ready to answer some more questions.

"Buddy?"

He looked up from his play, smiling. "This is a nice bear," he said. "Does he have a name?"

"Probably. I don't know what it is, though. Why don't you give him one of your own?"

"Can I?" he asked excitedly.

"Sure, go ahead."

I sighed and wandered back to the kitchen. I'd ask him about the murder again later.

Myra had left a half-full pot of cold coffee, so I heated it up. What I really craved was an Anchor Steam.

I called my answering machine to check for phone messages and was surprised to hear Philly Post's surly baritone.

"If you've got the kid, Ventana, you're dead."

Simple, honest, and to the point.

The next message was from Phoebe, an urgent "Call me. It's important."

I picked up the phone and dialed.

"Phoebe? It's Ronnie."

"Thank God. Where are you?"

"I'm not at home."

"The police think you've stolen Buddy Murphy. Scotch Morgan is doing everything he can to get a warrant. So far he's not having any luck, but I don't know how long that's going to hold. Anybody who has that kid should just drop him off someplace safe, like the hospital or his school," she said pointedly. "I hope that's what the kidnapper'll do, don't you?"

I glanced across the room at Buddy. He'd found a cup full of swizzle sticks and was lining them up on the coffee table according to color and size. "Mmm," I said.

"He's a material witness to a homicide," she said, and launched into her hundredth spiel about how serious everything was.

I let her rag on for a while, then said, "I know how bad things look, Phoebe. That's why I'm trying to find the real killer. I need some time, that's all."

"Then you'd better stay low, because if they find you, they're going to bring you in for questioning. They can hold you forty-eight hours every time they pick you up. And weekends don't count."

"Thanks."

I hung up and called Mitch, my ex, and arranged to borrow one of his cars. He lives in Marin, and my Toyota would be well hidden if I left it in his drive up in the woods on Mount Tam.

Myra finally rolled in around two-thirty.

"His picture is everywhere," she whispered as soon as she'd closed the door behind her. "This isn't going to work. You've got to get him out of here."

"Just keep him inside until I get back. I promise I won't be gone long."

"But—"

I grabbed my jacket and backpack, winked at Buddy, and waved a jaunty good-bye to Myra.

"Later, Buddy. I'll be back tonight and we'll head over to Blackie's, okay?"

"Blackie's! Yeah!" He clutched the now-crumpled, one-hundred-year-old teddy bear, grinned, and followed me out the door with his eyes.

CHAPTER

16

By SEVEN-THIRTY, I was tired and hungry. I'd traded my blue Toyota for Mitch's old Citroën, nosed around the Tenderloin, trying without any luck to get information about Sondra Murphy, then, around five o'clock, relieved Blackie on his stakeout.

One more hour, I told myself. Then I'd step out of the car and walk around inconspicuously to wake myself up. I started to yawn, then froze. A woman—the first Caucasian woman I'd seen in the neighborhood—walked by.

As she passed under the soft yellow glow of the streetlamp, I saw that her hair was a dirty brown, that her clothes were much too nice for this neighborhood, and that her body was emaciated. My Charlotte Murphy impersonator hadn't seemed skinny, but then maybe it had been her clothes.

She stopped in front of the Victorian, looked

briefly over her shoulder—too briefly for me to make out her face—then started up the steps.

I waited until she was at the door, then jumped out of my car, feeling suddenly wide awake and full of energy. I hurried across the street, past the wino lookouts, and up the stoop to stand behind her just as the door came open.

"Sondra," I said softly.

With her hand still on the doorknob, she turned haunted, drug-emptied eyes on me. Up close, you could see that the ravages of the street life had marked deep lines in her face. An open sore along her jaw line marred her once-pretty face.

This definitely wasn't the woman who'd impersonated Charlotte Murphy. But could she have killed her own father? She blinked at me.

"Are you Sondra Murphy?"

She shook her head and set one foot across the threshold.

"Are you Buddy's mom?" I asked.

She hesitated, then shook her head again and stepped inside. I followed her.

"Buddy's in a lot of pain right now," I said. "He'd like to see you."

She stopped midway to the stairs and turned to face me. Her expression was filled with a hard edginess but when she spoke, her voice trembled. "I'm not going to see him," she said. "Not now. Not like this. I can't handle it. I'm no good at this."

She started up the steps. A couple of grinning

Latino thugs were on their way down so we hugged the wall to let them pass.

"Sondra," I said when we reached the landing. She ignored me and started down the hall. I trailed after her.

"I'm not going to talk to you," she said when she stopped in front of a door and realized I'd followed.

"Just give me five minutes."

"Why should I?"

"Because talking to me beats talking to the police."

"They've been here already."

"Did you tell them you argued with your father before he died?"

Her eyes narrowed. "What do you want?"

"Five minutes."

She unlocked the door and walked in, not bothering to turn on the light but leaving the door open behind her.

I stepped into the darkened apartment and was instantly hit with a wall of moist, funky-smelling air that made me gag. The room smelled like some of the homeless people on the street.

I almost tripped over a junkie dozing on the floor as I followed Sondra Murphy into the kitchen. When she switched on the overhead bulb, a couple of strung-out women stumbled out of the room like cockroaches skittering from the light.

Sondra closed the kitchen door and faced me. I felt sorry for her. Her clothes spoke of a better time, a younger time, before drugs had turned her into an old woman. I stared deep into her eyes. Could she have killed her own father?

"Have you got any money?" she asked, reaching into her handbag. She pulled out a cigarette and dropped into a chair at the kitchen table. Cigarette smoke on top of this fetid air?

I crossed to the window above the cluttered sink and raised it. Before I returned to the table, I sucked in a couple of deep breaths just so my lungs wouldn't collapse. Then I walked over, sat down, and pulled out a twenty.

"I need to ask you a few questions about your father's death," I said, laying the bill on the table between us. I kept my fingers on it.

She eyed the cash like it was her salvation, then studied my face with her rheumy eyes. "Who are you? You're not a cop."

I wondered what the trail had been from that privileged, antique-filled house in Presidio Heights to this junkie-infested flat in the Mission. I reached inside my jacket with my free hand, pulled out a card, and set it on the table next to the twenty.

"I'm a private investigator. My name's Ronnie Ventana."

She glanced down at the card, then back at me. "You know Buddy?"

"That's right. When was the last time you saw your father?"

She sucked on her cigarette like it was oxygen. "It's been a while."

"Try Monday."

She blinked. "Monday? Yeah, I guess it was Monday." She reached up, scratched her face, and opened a sore on her chin. The blood just sort of sprang to the surface and sat there, glistening in the soft light. I focused on her eyes.

"Did you see him after that?"

"No."

"What did the two of you fight about?"

She stared, then shoved her chair back. The sound of the wood scraping against the floor sounded like a moan. She looked ready to jump out the window.

"No you don't," she said. "You think I killed him. That's what you're getting at, isn't it? Well, I didn't. I asked him for money. He said no. I left and I came home. And I didn't go back. Why would I kill him?"

"He refused to give you money."

She tried to summon some indignation but she seemed too tired. "I don't need to listen to this," she said wearily. "Not in my own house."

I raised the twenty-dollar bill. She snatched it and buried it inside her soiled blouse. "You got your money's worth. Now, go! Go before I—"

"Call the police?" I didn't move.

"We've got our own kind of cops down here."

"And I'll bet they'd be thrilled to know who's been cooperating with the cops."

"That's a lie."

"They won't know that."

She smashed her cigarette out on a dirty plate

on the table. "What do you want? I didn't kill him, okay? I didn't do it and I don't know who did."

"Fine. Then you shouldn't mind helping me find the real killer. What did you two really argue about?"

She sighed. "I told you: money. And Buddy."

"What about Buddy?"

"Dad wanted me to sign into detox so I could clean up and take care of Buddy. It's always the same old dance. Buddy doesn't need me."

"He needs a responsible guardian."

"Yeah, well." She spread her spindly arms. "Look around. That's not me."

I wasn't going to disagree. "So your father tried to get you into detox."

"It was the same thing every time I went over there. I should have known he hadn't given up. I thought he was going to give me some cash this time, but it was the same old trap." She sighed. "Look at this place. I can't believe he cut me off the way he did. Nothing. He's given me absolutely nothing since I moved out."

"Are you in his will?"

"He'd rather flush it down the toilet than leave anything to me. It's all in a trust for Buddy. He set up a trust a long time ago."

"Who's the executor?"

She shrugged. "Not me."

"Can you think of anybody who'd want to kill your father?"

She sneered. "You mean besides me?"

"Besides you."

She reached for another cigarette. Her long, white fingers shook.

"Was he seeing anybody?"

"You mean like dating?"

I nodded.

"Think he'd tell me if he was?"

"Do you know a woman who has dark hair, a turned-up nose, about my height, and a little heavier? She wears expensive clothes. Shops at Montague's Trap and Saddle."

"What do you think?" Sondra Murphy lit the cigarette, tilted her head, and sat there smoking for so long that I thought she'd forgotten me.

"There *was* something," she finally said. "A chick—she didn't look like who you're talking about—but she showed up here one night. I thought she was with a friend of mine but when I asked him later, he thought she was with me. Nobody knew who she was but she had some good dope so we knew she wasn't a cop. She kept passing me dope and asking about Dad."

I sat up. "What did she want to know?"

It was a mistake to show my interest. Sondra wiggled her fingers for more cash. I shelled out another twenty and waited.

"She asked was I close to him, what would he do if I OD'd, would he be torn up, would he ransom me if I was kidnapped. All I could do was laugh. My dad wouldn't lift a finger to save my life even if his own life depended on it. Then I told her about Buddy."

"What about Buddy?"

"That if she *really* wanted to get to Dad, she needed to use Buddy."

"You told her that?"

She looked up sharply, hearing the anger in my voice. "Yeah," she said, her tone defensive and cold as she stubbed out her cigarette and lit another one. "Something wrong with that?"

I couldn't believe she was so stupid. "You gave her an open invitation to harm Buddy," I said.

"It was an invitation to harm *Dad*," she answered. "Funny. This chick was the first thing that popped into my head when I heard Dad was dead."

I asked her to describe the woman but she couldn't even remember the color of her hair. "Did you tell the police?"

"Are you crazy? What am I going to tell them? They'd be all over my neck till I told them where to find her. I don't know who she is. I'd never seen her before and I haven't seen her since."

Down the hall the front door opened. As heavy steps crossed the floor toward us, she seemed to come alive and gather confidence. She smiled at me through the smoke. "And don't you ask me where she is. Can't help you," she said as a hulking biker type barged into the kitchen.

"Who's she?" he demanded, turning red-rimmed eyes from her to me. "You a narc?"

Sondra picked up the card I'd tossed on the table. "She's a private cop. Asking about my dead dad." She snorted. "Like anybody cares."

The gorilla stepped into the room. He smelled of sweat and booze. "We don't talk to cops," he growled. "No kind of cops."

I ignored the thug and leaned across the table toward Sondra. "Buddy needs you," I said.

"Yeah?" She stubbed out her second cigarette and leveled her suddenly dead eyes at me. "He'll get over it."

CHAPTER

17

WHEN I PULLED onto Myra's block, I knew instantly that something had gone wrong. The place was crawling with cop cars.

I slowed the Citroën and pulled around a double-parked black-and-white, saw a uniformed policewoman at somebody's front door a few houses down from Myra's and a TV crew down the street and decided to keep going.

There was a phone booth on Lombard, by a video store, so I stopped there and dialed Myra.

"What's going on?" I asked when she picked up.

"Can you call back later? I've got—uh—visitors right now."

"The police?"

"Yes."

"Where's Buddy?"

"He went out? Well, he's not here. I don't know where Daddy went."

"Don't tell them anything," I said, then hung up.

I fished another pair of dimes out of my pocket and dialed the Quarter Moon. The bartender's deep bass voice bellowed into the telephone. "Yo!"

"Marcus? Ronnie. How's it look?"

"Perfect," he said. "Just perfect."

I found Blackie at the Perfect Pub out on Geary. It was our alternate meeting place when the Quarter Moon was too hot. Blackie was playing liar's dice with the bartender, but when I came in, he followed me to a table in the corner.

The place was pretty much empty except for a couple of gray-haired men in the back trading shots at a dartboard.

After delivering a pair of fresh, cold Anchor Steams, the bartender went back to the bar and used the remote to turn up the volume on the television that hung from the ceiling. As he did, a picture of Buddy came on the screen.

". . . continues. Clarence 'Buddy' Murphy, the mentally impaired grandson of the late Senator Payton Murphy, who was believed to have been kidnapped from Stickley Convalescent Hospital last night, was found wandering alone in Pacific Heights this afternoon. Police refused to speculate, but a source close to the department said officials are considering the possibility that Murphy was not kidnapped after all but in fact wandered away from the hospital of his own volition."

"Keep thinking that way," I muttered.

"Looks like your cousin fucked up," Blackie said.

"Well, at least he went back in a lot better shape than when I found him. Maybe they won't dope him up now."

The news report moved on to something else and Blackie turned away from the television to face me. He reached for a cigarette from his breast pocket and lit it.

"Your lady turn up?"

I nodded. "She wasn't my impostor. And if she knows anything, she's not telling."

"She in the will?"

"Out without a dime. It's all in a trust for Buddy."

"She'll be pretty popular down there for a while, at least until they find out Buddy inherits Payton Murphy's estate."

"She'll still get some of it."

Blackie blew smoke into the room. "How do you figure?"

"She'll hit Buddy up for it. You heard him. She throws the old 'mom loves you' business at him and he's bound to be giving her a lot of it. Even with a guardian." I stood. "I've got to make a call," I said, and headed toward the back.

When Phoebe Wright picked up the phone and recognized my voice, she sounded exasperated.

"Where are you?" she demanded.

"I'm fine. How are you?"

"The police want you to come in for a lineup. They've found Buddy Murphy and—"

"What if I don't come in?"

"Ronnie—you've got to stop acting like a renegade. They'll arrest you and things will be more difficult than they need to be. Scotch Morgan will see to that. If you come in now and they charge you, I'm pretty sure I can convince the judge to give you bail. If you wait, though, I can't make any promises."

I thought a moment. I could keep avoiding the police or I could go in and get it over with. Buddy might or might not I.D. me. If he did, and if Phoebe came through and got me out, I could keep investigating without trying to keep such a low profile. My life would be easier.

"Well?" she asked.

"Do you know who'll be Buddy's guardian now that Payton Murphy's dead?"

"What?"

"I need to know."

"If I tell you, will you come in?"

"Sure."

"Dr. Patel. Dr. Miranda Patel."

"I'll be there in an hour," I said, and hung up before she could object.

Blackie had ordered fresh Anchor Steams while I was on the phone.

"What's the story?" he asked as I sat down across from him again.

"Buddy's guardian?" I said.

"Yeah?"

"Dr. Miranda Patel."

"The shrink?"

"I'd like to find out more about her. Have you ever dated a shrink, Blackie?"

He grinned and winked broadly. "They got the best couches, doll."

I thought of Buddy. "This probably means he's got to stay in the hospital."

We both stared at the table. I couldn't stop thinking of the dazed kid I'd found wandering the streets.

"Poor bastard," Blackie finally said, raising his beer to his lips. I downed half the bottle in a long slug and said, "The police want me to stand a lineup."

Blackie set his empty on the table. "He'll make you, doll. You just spent a whole day with him."

"I know. My lawyer says she can get me out."

Blackie snorted. "You're already out."

CHAPTER 18

"NUMBER TWO, step forward, please."

The voice from the intercom sounded tinny. I took one step forward and stared at the one-way glass on the opposite wall.

Blackie's logic had been sound as far as I was concerned, but I'd gone in anyway. I'd lived with my parents long enough to learn there's nothing worse than being wanted by the law.

"Turn to the right," the voice said.

I did.

"Step back."

Silence. Then, "Number Four, step forward, please."

It went like that for a quick five minutes, then they led me into a tiny room with a table and two chairs and left me there without an explanation. Seconds later, Phoebe burst in.

"Did you kidnap him?" she demanded.

I let her wait a beat. "I thought lawyers aren't supposed to ask clients questions like that?"

She slapped her briefcase onto the floor and dropped into the empty chair in front of me. "Buddy Murphy says he knows you. Didn't I tell you not to talk to him?"

"I saw him wandering around and I gave him a ride. I bought him dinner. That's not kidnapping."

"They're not charging you with kidnapping yet. They've got bigger problems right now."

"What? Scotch Morgan wants to give me the electric chair?"

"Worse. Buddy confessed."

"To what?"

"He says *he* killed his grandfather."

"*Buddy?* No way. That's crazy."

"He says Ronnie told him to do it. That's why they wanted the lineup. Scotch Morgan thought he had you. But then Buddy said it wasn't you; it was another Ronnie. Do you know who he's talking about?"

"No."

Phoebe stared hard at me like she was trying to decide whether to believe me or not.

"He knows you, Ronnie. He calls you Ronnie Vee. He says 'just plain Ronnie' told him to throw the radio in the tub. Says she told him since Payton loves music, he'd really love the music in the tub."

"What are you saying?" I wasn't sure I understood.

"I mean someone conned Buddy into electrocuting his own grandfather."

"Jesus." I collapsed against the back of my chair, feeling like a cement truck had landed on my chest. "But . . . Buddy wouldn't do anything like that. Not unless he didn't realize what he was doing."

"That's what Dr. Patel contends. Scotch says she told him Buddy's knowledge about stuff like that's pretty specific. He knows hair dryers and electric shavers are no-nos, but somebody forgot to include radios. And he can't translate from one to the other or draw inferences like that. He didn't know that's what would happen. In fact Ronnie—the other Ronnie—convinced him the old man would love it."

I tried to picture the kind of creep who'd do that to a kid like Buddy. "What's going to happen to him?"

"Well, the D.A.'s walking on eggshells. We're talking about a senator's murder and a senator's grandson. Plus he's mentally handicapped. The D.A.'s not sure which direction the political wind is blowing, so he's taking things very slowly. He just released Buddy into Dr. Patel's custody and she took him back to the hospital for tonight."

"Are they charging him?"

"Not yet. I don't think they know what to do. Buddy's obviously pretty confused about what's what. Dr. Patel says Ronnie doesn't exist. She says he made her up. But did he know he was committing murder? She says no way, but Scotch isn't buying it. He's ready to nail Buddy. I think he'd rather do that than just sit there licking his wounds. But the D.A.'s stepped in and told Scotch to lighten up." She shook her head and her curls bounced like wire coils. "Scotch thought he had you cold until Buddy said you weren't the right Ronnie."

"Is Scotch Morgan still here?"

Phoebe frowned. "Why?"

"I want to talk to him."

"That's not a good idea, Ronnie."

"What's she look like, this other Ronnie?"

Phoebe hesitated, then looked straight into my eyes. "Just like you," she said. "Almost exactly like you."

CHAPTER
19

I SAID, "DON'T YOU SEE? They're the same person."

Scotch Morgan laughed like he'd just heard the funniest joke in the world. We were in his modest, civil-service-equipped office which he'd upgraded by bringing in his own mahogany desk and a leather-upholstered executive chair that squeaked every time he leaned back. Phoebe sat rigidly at my side like a disapproving, wire-haired sphinx. I tried again.

"The woman who hired me—the one who told me she was Charlotte Murphy—and the woman who told Buddy she was Ronnie are one and the same. He didn't make her up, Mr. Morgan. She's very real and very deadly."

Scotch stopped laughing.

"Okay," he said. "Just for the sake of argument, let's say she *does* exist." Morgan shuffled through the papers in a file folder on his desk.

In a corner of the room was a black briefcase

with a racquetball racquet sticking out at an angle. Behind his desk were certificates from college and law school—Hastings—and a bunch of soccer trophies. Scotch yanked a sheet out and read from it.

"Caucasian. Five-five or -six. One-thirty, maybe one-forty. Green eyes. Dark hair. Turned-up nose. Pierced ears. Late twenties, early thirties."

He set the paper down and leaned back. The chair squeaked. "That's your description of alias Charlotte Murphy. Buddy Murphy says *his* person looks just like you. Have you looked in the mirror lately?"

Next to me Phoebe stirred. "The differences aren't great enough to rule out the possibility that they could be the same person," she said. "Ronnie's got brown eyes and her nose isn't turned up. She's a little lighter too. But—"

Morgan shook his head. "The good Dr. Patel says Murphy's friend is make-believe and that's good enough for me." He brought his predatory little eyes to rest on mine. "Why don't you just admit you invented Charlotte Murphy?"

Phoebe lunged forward in her seat. "That's enough," she snapped, and started gathering up her things. "Come on, Ronnie. We don't need to listen to this."

Something in her tone made me glance at her. The set of her mouth and the way she squinted her eyes at me were the same as when she'd bluff at poker.

I stayed where I was. "If I admitted that I made her up, I'd be lying, Mr. Morgan. I've been telling you the truth all along. The woman who calls herself Charlotte Murphy bought a scarf at Montague's Trap and Saddle on Maiden Lane. They keep records of their sales. Why don't you check it out?"

Scotch Morgan pulled a long face like I'd just insulted him. "I know what went down, lady. You conned the kid into murdering his old man—"

"That's a lie," I said through gritted teeth.

Morgan kept on talking. "You had Buddy Murphy do the killing because you didn't think we would prosecute him. You made up this Charlotte Murphy business, and now you're trying to send us on a wild-goose chase after somebody you and Buddy Murphy invented. Guess what, Ms. Ventana. I'm not buying it."

He rested his head against the back of his chair and hooked his stout little thumbs under his suspenders. He looked satisfied with himself.

"We know that's what happened," Morgan continued, "so why don't you just admit it and make things easier for everybody?"

"What's my motive?"

Phoebe's eyes hardened, but I was the only one who noticed. Scotch grinned.

"He dumped you," he said.

"I never met Payton Murphy."

"Want to bet?"

"I'll swear to it under oath."

"You'd be committing perjury, Ms. Ventana. We've got witnesses, witnesses that'll testify you two met last May. We've even got pictures of the two of you together holding hands."

"That's impossible."

Scotch rummaged through his file folder and pulled out an eight-by-ten black-and-white glossy. With a satisfied smirk, he slid it across the desktop. Phoebe and I both grabbed it at once.

I was in running shorts and T-shirt, crouched over a prone figure on the pavement. My face was turned toward the camera and we were surrounded by a wall of legs, hairy men's legs. There was a date stamped in the lower right-hand side of the picture.

"Is that you?" Morgan asked.

"Don't answer that," Phoebe said.

"This is the Bay to Breakers," I said, then pointed to the guy on the pavement, the one whose hand I was holding. "This guy was running ahead of me and had a heart attack. I stopped to help."

I remembered the man's face vividly. He didn't even resemble the pictures I'd seen of Senator Murphy. But then he'd just had a heart attack when I saw him.

Morgan slid a photocopy of the picture and caption from the newspaper over to me. It identified the prone man as Senator Payton Murphy. "Do you deny knowing him now?"

"Five minutes, ten minutes max till the ambulance came. I didn't know who it was."

"Who's going to believe you saved a senator's life and didn't know it?"

"I got caught up in a murder investigation the next day. I didn't know it was Murphy."

"Think a jury will buy that? We've got you at the scene, we've got your connection to the victim, and we've got the kid saying, 'Ronnie told me to do it.'"

"And the Doctor saying that's make-believe," Phoebe added.

Morgan dismissed her with a careless wave of his hand. "The preponderance of the evidence is on my side."

"Book her, then," Phoebe said. "Arrest her."

My jaw dropped. *"Phoebe!"*

My lawyer glanced at me, then back at Morgan. "Go ahead, Scotch. *Arrest* her."

I knew Phoebe was playing lawyer games. And I knew she was good at it. But the smell of the crowded holding cell was still too fresh in my mind. "I don't think—"

Without taking her eyes off Morgan, Phoebe raised her hand to silence me. "Well?" she demanded.

By now Morgan's face was starting to flush. His neck quivered and I thought he was about to burst.

"Go ahead," Phoebe urged. Her voice was as gentle and enticing as a kitten's purr.

Morgan jerked his eyes away from Phoebe and

brought them to rest on me. They were full of anger and hatred and testosterone.

"You're mine," he whispered, then hoisted himself out of his chair and left us sitting in his empty office.

CHAPTER

20

THE FIRST THING I did when I found out they weren't going to hold me was phone Blackie.

"Charlotte Murphy set me and Buddy up," I told him. "She killed the Senator and set us both up. It's a setup inside a setup."

"What happened to the kid?"

"They took him back to the hospital."

"Fuck."

"Listen, Blackie. Buddy told them somebody calling herself Ronnie—somebody with dark hair like mine, about my build—told him to throw the radio into the old man's bath. Said he liked music so much, he'd love the music in the water."

Blackie swore again. "We'll find her, doll. We'll find her and fry her for good."

But I didn't have a clue where to look. Trap and Saddle might have sales records, but I didn't have enough information to recognize the right name even if I saw it.

I'd gone back to the restaurant and the parking

garages without any luck. I'd talked to Buddy and I'd talked to his mother. I'd been through the society pages and to the Old Maids' dance. I'd even gotten Aldo to show me the crime-scene photos. All without turning up a thing. I felt like I'd never even left square one.

Square one. That was the answer.

"How do you feel about a little B-and-E?" I asked.

Blackie's mind was working right along with mine. "Murphy's house?"

"You know what they say, second time's the charm."

CHAPTER

21

I'D SPENT SO much time in Payton Murphy's house last Tuesday night that I almost felt at home. I knew where the control unit for the burglar alarm was, I knew what brand it was, and I knew the cops had probably left it turned off.

We went in through a side window this time—police seals were on all the doors—and found the den. It was on the north side of the house, toward the back, so we wouldn't have to worry about our flashlights being seen from the street. But we did have to worry about the neighbors.

I pulled the curtains shut, then flipped on my penlight and looked around. Blackie did the same. We were surrounded by antiques—exquisite, gilded antiques.

"Fuckin' museum," Blackie muttered.

I took the desk while Blackie circled the room, lifting paintings away from the walls in search of a safe. I went through the lap drawer, but all I found were bills and invoices, a checkbook and ledger.

I scanned the ledger. Nothing jumped out at me. Payton Murphy had written checks to the gas company, a housekeeping service, the burglar-alarm company. The last check written was to a department store and the balance was $10,052.

Across the room Blackie gave up on finding a wall safe and started rummaging through the file cabinets. They were disguised as an old oak side-board.

I moved on in my search through the desk. There was a fifth of vodka in the bottom drawer and a pistol complete with permit and a box of bullets. The next drawer held a bunch of corre-spondence. I paged through it but nothing jumped out at me. I closed the drawer and sighed. *All right, then. Mom? Dad? Where to now?*

At the sideboard, Blackie grunted. Crossing the shadows toward where I sat, he said, "Take a look at this, doll."

He tossed a thick file folder onto the desk. I picked it up, read the letters on the tab.

"BOPT." My heart leaped. "Board of Prison Terms."

"They the guns you used to work for?"

"Sort of."

There were acres and acres of middle manage-ment between parole officers and the board, the dozen high-minded, upright citizens appointed to pass final judgment on whether parolees deserve parole or not and for how long.

I opened the folder. The familiar BOPT letter-head jumped out at me. The first page was a letter dated nine years ago, signed Edgar L. Moffet, Commissioner. Moffett congratulated Murphy on his appointment to lieutenant governor and thanked him for serving the last nine months on the board as a deputy commissioner.

"Maybe Scotch Morgan's right," I said.

Blackie frowned. "You crazy, doll? What are you talking about?"

"No, no, listen to this. Scotch Morgan thinks there's some kind of connection between me and Payton Murphy. He's trying to work up some bo-gus Bay to Breakers deal, but this—this could be the real thing, Blackie. According to this, Payton Murphy was on the board when I was a parole officer."

There was too much in the folder to read here. I closed it and stood. "Anything else in that cabi-net about BOPT?"

Blackie crossed back to the sideboard and flashed his tiny penlight around. "Nah."

I checked my watch. We'd been inside fifteen minutes—ten minutes more than we should have been. As I slipped the desk chair back to where I'd found it, Blackie started for the window.

"Hold on, Blackie. I've got to run upstairs a minute."

I tossed him the folder and rushed up to find Buddy's room. It was easy—cowboy curtains, a few scattered toys on the floor, and MUNI bus maps pasted all over his walls. The room was comfortable and straightforwardly simple, like Buddy. His tin candy box, the one with the eagle on it, was on his dresser. I grabbed it, stuffed it inside my jacket, and ran back downstairs to the den.

"Let's get out of here, Blackie. We've got some reading to do."

CHAPTER 22

I HANDED THE last page from the folder to Blackie and reached for the bottle of Anchor Steam on the table I use for a desk. It was empty.

I got up, stretched, and pulled two cold, fresh ones out of the fridge. I took a healthy swig out of one, then set the other one down in front of Blackie just as he tossed the last page onto the stack on the floor at his feet.

"Fuckin' bureaucrats," he said, then raised the beer to his lips and drank.

I sank back into the chair behind the table and stared at the stack of papers the BOPT had generated. It started with a letter confirming Payton Murphy's appointment to the board, his salary—which was three times what the P.O.'s got paid—and his general obligations.

The rest were notices of salary increases, board meetings, new appointments to the board, and a bunch of political stuff that seemed fairly meaningless and reminded me of the eternal stream of stupid memos that had appeared on my desk at the parole office.

"Maybe she's an ex-parolee of mine," I said. "And she must have crossed paths with Murphy too."

Not too tough since anybody who got revoked had the right to automatically appeal the revocation all the way up to the deputy commissioners. And this file showed in black and white that Payton Murphy had been a commissioner on the board for nine months.

Blackie reached into his shirt pocket, pulled out a pack of cigarettes, and tapped one out. He lit it slowly, then as he blew smoke into the air, he said, "Outta how many we talkin' about, doll?"

"I probably covered a couple of hundred parolees in the two years I was there."

"Fuck."

"They weren't all my enemies. I liked most of them and most of them liked me."

Blackie narrowed his eyes and squinted at me through the smoke drifting in front of his face. "Didn't you get fired for loansharking those guys?"

"I didn't get fired, Blackie. When I left, it was mutual."

He shrugged. "Whatever."

"And I never loansharked anybody. It would have been loansharking if I had charged them interest and broken their legs when they didn't pay me back. All I did was lend a few parolees some money—just to tide them over. Sometimes all these guys need is a break.''

Blackie washed down any objection he might have had with a determined slug of Anchor Steam. "So besides the guys you worked for, those commissioners, who were the assholes?''

I found a scrap of paper, made a list of possible subjects, and showed them to Blackie.

He squinted at the list. "Five? That's all the enemies you made in two years of sending guys back to the slammer? Get serious, doll.''

"I tried not to send anybody back. I recommended probation for the ones I could and kept the others out on parole the best I could. These—'' I pointed to the paper between us. "These are the ones I sent back. They were basically incorrigible.''

There were two women and three men on the list. Women don't commit as many crimes, so I'd decided to be open-minded and include men. Charlotte Murphy could be an accomplice, a front, for a guy I'd easily recognize.

Blackie glanced down and read the first name. "Julius Brown. What was his rap?''

"Manslaughter. He killed a couple of immigrant shopkeepers in the Sunset and the P.D. pleaded him down to manslaughter. I revoked him because he robbed a convenience store the third day he was out.''

"Ever threaten you?''

"They all do.''

Blackie looked down at the list again. "Harris Windsor."

"Harry was weird. He was quiet and polite, but you could tell there was something really wrong with him, some kind of rage boiling inside. I revoked him when he put his eighty-three-year-old dad in the hospital with a broken jaw and seven cracked ribs. Dad was too scared to talk, but nobody was buying the 'He fell out of his wheelchair' routine."

"Fuckin' loser," Blackie muttered, then read the third name. "Sara Girard?"

"I felt sorry for her." Like I did most of the women parolees I'd come across. "She got sucked into the gang culture and made some big mistakes. She and her boyfriend supposedly killed six rival gang members. I don't think she killed anybody, but her P.D. couldn't talk her out of sharing the blame. It was some kind of gang code or something. She did okay on parole until her boyfriend got out. For their first date they hit a gas station and they both went back."

"What'd she look like?"

I pictured the acne-scarred face of the sullen young woman who'd sulked through every contact we'd had and I shook my head.

"Not even close." No way she could have passed herself off as a society girl.

He moved down the list. "Hilda Nuñez."

"Same thing. A gang story. Shot her rival for a drug lord's affection. When she got out, she started harassing the drug lord's family. She needed help, more than she could get on the out-side. I sent her back before her ex lost his patience and decided to kill her. She couldn't be Charlotte Murphy for the same reason Sara Girard couldn't—too rough around the edges."

I glanced at the last name on the list. "And you already saw Dwight Baker," I said.

"Asshole at your cousin's party?"

"Right. He beat up his high school sweetheart, almost killed her. He raped a woman a few months after he got out, so I revoked him. Gladly."

"Where's the BOPT come in?"

"It's possible one of these five pulled Payton Murphy for their revocation hearing. The deputy commissioners have got the final word. There are around twelve of them, but you only get one or two for a hearing."

Blackie studied the list. "No probationers?"

"Judges decide what to do with them. BOPT has nothing to do with probationers." I tapped my list. "There may be others I've forgotten, but these are the guys who stand out. I'll ask Edna—"

Blackie frowned.

"—my friend at the parole office, remember? I'll ask her to look into her computer files. Maybe she can tell me if I forgot anybody. Or if any of these guys drew Payton Murphy for their revocation hearing."

Once Blackie was gone, I glanced at the clock by the sofa bed. It was a quarter past two.

My eyes fell on the eagle-imprinted tin I'd

stolen from Buddy's room and I wondered if Buddy was asleep now, if he'd been sedated again, or if they'd seen he was doing all right without the drugs and had left him alone. I reached over and touched the tin.

"Hold on, Buddy," I whispered to the empty room. "Hold on."

CHAPTER 23

I'D BEEN ALL the way to Fort Point and was running back along Crissy Field the next morning before I realized it was Sunday. Edna wouldn't be in her office today—unless I could convince her to be.

When I got back, I showered and then dialed Edna at home. She picked up on the second ring. Twenty minutes later I had agreed to beef up her mother-in-law's security system in exchange for all-day access to the parole-office files.

"I'll meet you there in an hour," I said, and hung up. My doorbell buzzed.

I checked my watch. Nine o'clock. Too early for Blackie. I crossed over to the window, raised it, and peered down at the sidewalk below.

A woman, slight in build, blond, and vaguely familiar, waited by the front door. She didn't look dangerous. But then neither had Ted Bundy. I grabbed the hammer from under the sink and buzzed her in.

As she came up the stairs, she glanced up. Katherine, the salesclerk from the Trap and Saddle.

"Hello," she said solemnly.

She paused at the top of the steps and stared at my hand. That's when I remembered my fingers were still wrapped firmly around the hammer.

"I'm doing some plumbing work," I lied, then motioned for her to come inside.

Katherine stood in the middle of the room, scoping the place out and pretending not to while I came around and set the hammer on the table. She was average in size but had long limbs, catlike eyes, and a sullen kind of sensuality I hadn't noticed at the shop or on the bus. Today she struck me as sort of like a female James Dean.

I asked her to sit, then took the chair behind the table. "What can I do for you, Katherine?"

She stopped scanning the room, sat down like she thought the chair might explode, and crossed her arms. Her mouth formed a perfect, unconscious pout, which vanished when she offered me a weak but conciliatory smile. She seemed scared.

"You said you wanted some information," she finally said.

I crossed my arms and regarded her for a minute. "You didn't seem too anxious to give me any on the bus the other day. What's changed your mind?"

She bit her lip. "I've had time to think. Have you ever worked for somebody like Cedric?"

I shrugged. "Probably. He's a jerk, right?"

"Cedric is a royal ass. And I'd very much enjoy

screwing him over—as long as he doesn't find out. Can you promise me he won't?"

"No."

She raised her finely etched eyebrows in surprise. "Will you at least try to keep him from finding out?"

"Sure. But I can't make any guarantees."

She seemed to think it over, then shrugged. "Oh, well, it'll be worth it."

We sat there eyeing each other for a couple of seconds. Then I finally asked, "What have you got?"

Katherine hesitated, then smiled for the first time. "What do you want?"

"I need to find a woman who bought a Siven scarf—one with the pastel blues and oranges."

"We sell a lot of those scarves."

I described my Charlotte Murphy. "Have you sold one to a woman fitting that description?"

Katherine shifted in her seat and crossed her long legs. "It's hard to say. Maybe. What was she wearing? That's all I'd really notice."

"Her clothes would have been expensive."

She sighed. "This is going to be harder than I thought. They all wear expensive clothes. That's how they dress when they shop."

"Does the store keep records of its sales?"

"Sure. Cedric's got a card for every client."

I tried to keep the excitement from my voice. "Every client?"

"Everybody. Their size, color preference, and everything they've ever bought. Plus stuff like,

'Mrs. Davison has a white poodle named Cherché and a husband who heads Bank National West. Mrs. So-and-so likes Godiva chocolates and travels to Gstaad every year with her niece.' Those cards have got all kinds of details."

"Do you have access to them?"

"Sure. Cedric's constantly telling me I need to study them."

"Can you bring the cards home?"

"Oh, no. He wouldn't let them out of his sight. Those cards are his Bible."

"How about if you copy the names and addresses of the women who bought that scarf? Do you think you can do that?"

"He keeps a pretty close eye on me most of the time, but I can try."

"How soon can you have it?"

"I'll call you," she said, looking solemn and satisfied as she tucked my card into her designer handbag and walked out the door.

CHAPTER

24

I SPENT THE best part of Sunday afternoon wandering through a labyrinth of computerized parole records while Edna zipped through her backlog of paperwork. She even made a few phone calls, and surprised some parolees, who were probably, if things hadn't changed, happy to hear from her. Edna's the perfect parole officer: She's the kind of person everybody wants to please.

By three o'clock I was exhausted. Every familiar name I pulled up on the computer screen meant a memory, either good or bad, but mostly bad. Pathetic, messed-up people trying to make it without a chance. The afternoon had been an emotional roller coaster.

I was staring at the blank spot where Joe Danner's name would be if he were out on parole when Edna came up behind me.

"You've been staring at that screen without moving for fifteen minutes," she said. "Thinking about Danner?"

"Every once in a while I wonder how he's doing."

"You should go see him."

I shook my head. "There's nothing to say."

Edna squeezed my shoulder. "You did your best, Ronnie. Sometimes things just don't work out."

I pressed a button to advance the screen. Edna kept on talking.

"He was innocent the first time, Ronnie, but the second time—"

"The second time was self-defense. He was defending himself from assault, an assault he never would have faced if he hadn't been revoked."

"You didn't revoke him, Ronnie. Vernon Russo did."

The idiot go-by-the-book P.O. who'd turned Danner in to the commission.

Edna looked at me with such pure sympathy that I felt a catch in my throat.

"It wasn't your fault." She squeezed my shoulder one last time, then gestured toward the screen and asked in a lighter voice, "What have you found? Anything?"

"According to this, only one of my five suspects is out on parole."

There were actually six revoked parolees if I counted Danner. I hadn't considered him last night, but I did today. I felt lousy even thinking such a thing and was relieved his name hadn't shown up in the computer.

"Who?"

"Dwight Baker."

Edna's delicate brows furrowed above her clear, almond-shaped eyes. "He's out? Good grief."

I tapped the keyboard. "Can I get the complete file on this thing?"

"It's abbreviated."

"Will it say which deputy commissioner upheld the revocation?"

"For that you've got to talk to his P.O. He can look it up in the hard-copy file. This'll tell us who's his P.O. May I?"

Edna took my chair and typed Dwight Baker's name. We stared at the pulsing orange text that materialized on the screen. Scooting to one side so I could see, she pointed to a name in the left-hand corner.

"Brigg Sturdevant," she said. "Do you know him? Was he here when you were?"

"Sure," I said with a smile. Brigg Sturdevant was a middle-aged man with the heart of a jolly prankster and really bad taste in clothes. He was a strictly Monday-through-Friday kind of guy.

"Brigg's got the complete file, but this will give you the basics. Here, take a look. Baker was released six months ago. Um, tony address. Pacific Heights, isn't it?"

Jackson Street. By the size of the house number, I knew it was on the west end, where the cramped apartment buildings give way to roomier condos, then to even larger houses.

"Where's he working?" I asked, peering at the screen. Every parolee needs to have a job.

Edna's slender finger touched the screen. "Stock boy slash kitchen help. Stickley Convalescent. Have you heard of it?"

CHAPTER

25

THE PART-TIME skeleton crew was on for Sunday afternoon at Stickley Convalescent, otherwise I never would have gotten in. I'd stopped by my apartment and gift-wrapped Buddy's candy tin, then dressed in khaki shorts, tennis shoes, and an I Love S.F. T-shirt so I'd look like a tourist.

Then I drove over to Stickley.

"You're his cousin?" the woman at the front door asked. Her guard uniform fit her perfectly, and she even had a badge and a nightstick but somehow she still managed to look an awful lot like Wally and Beaver's mom, Mrs. Cleaver.

"I'm just in town for the day," I explained. "And I've got a six-o'clock flight in the morning. I know you've got rules about visiting hours, but I wanted to say hi, you know, and give him my condolences."

Mrs. Cleaver's expression softened. "He's the one who lost his grandfather?"

I sighed dramatically. "Dear Uncle Payton."

The guard gave me a clipped but sympathetic nod and said, "Wait here."

Five minutes later she led me into a visiting room with upholstered chairs clustered at one end and some regular chairs around a small conference table at the other. Buddy bounded toward me like a big puppy.

"Ronnie Vee!" he shouted, and threw his arms around me. The security guard winked as she gently closed the door.

Buddy let go, then looked expectantly at the door. "Where's Blackie? Didn't Blackie come?"

"He couldn't make it, Buddy, but he says hi. How are you, Buddy?" I stepped back and studied his eyes. They were clear, not dilated. Good.

"I want to go home," he said. Then his gaze fell to the package in my hand. "Is that for me, Ronnie Vee?"

I gave it to him and he tore the paper savagely.

"Oh, boy!" he shouted when he saw the tin. He lifted the lid and pulled out a candy bar. He started to close the box, then stopped. "You want one, Ronnie Vee? You want one of my candy bars? You can have one if you want."

"Thanks, Buddy. You go ahead."

He looked relieved and devoured the chocolate in two quick gulps. Then he sat there at the little conference table smiling at me and hugging the tin box to his chest.

"I've got to ask you some questions, Buddy, so pay attention."

He nodded as his gaze wandered to a Peaceable Kingdom painting on the wall.

"There's a man who works here at Stickley, Buddy. His name is Dwight Baker."

"Dwight? That's a funny name."

"Do you know him, Buddy? Have you ever met anybody here named Dwight?"

He didn't answer. Instead he reached for the lid on the candy box.

"Buddy?"

He froze. "Yeah?"

"Do you know a man called Dwight Baker? He works in the kitchen." I described him.

"Uh-uh. Can I have another candy bar?"

"If you answer this next question first, okay?"

"Okay."

"You talked to the police yesterday, remember?"

He bobbed his head up and down. "They were real nice. That Mr. Morgan, he's a nice man. He gave me a hot chocolate."

"You told him about the radio, that somebody told you to throw that radio in the tub. Is that right?"

Buddy nodded again, this time a little less enthusiastically. His eyes fell to the table and he kept them there.

"Who told you to throw the radio in the bathtub?"

"Ronnie did."

"Not Dwight?"

"Huh-uh. It was Ronnie. I guess she didn't

know it wasn't no good. Maybe she didn't know it 'cause she's imaginary.''

"Do you know what 'imaginary' means, Buddy?''

He hunched his shoulders and smiled to hide his embarrassment. "Does it mean she forgets sometimes?''

"No, Buddy. 'Imaginary' means you made her up, that she's sort of like your dreams. Dreams are all in your head.''

"Oh.''

"Did you make up Ronnie? Is she all in your head, or is she real?''

Buddy seemed to think for a minute, then nodded. "Yeah," he said with conviction.

I took a deep breath and tried not to show my frustration.

"What is it about Ronnie that makes you say she's imaginary?''

" 'Cause Dr. Patel says she is. Can I have my candy bar now?''

"You're sure it wasn't Dwight Baker who told you to toss the radio in?''

"Nuh-huh.'' He eyed the tin.

"Did Ronnie have a boyfriend?''

Buddy blushed and looked away.

"Buddy? Did she?''

"She said I was her best man. Can I have my candy now, Ronnie Vee?''

He wolfed the second one down faster than he had the first.

"That was a good one. I think I like the ones with the peanuts best."

"Say, Buddy, can you take me to Ronnie? Do you know where she lives?"

"Huh-uh." He stroked the tin absently. I could tell he wanted a third candy bar but was afraid to ask.

"How did you meet her?" I asked.

"She was riding the bus. She gave me a candy bar."

"I thought you weren't supposed to talk to strangers."

"She wasn't no stranger, Ronnie Vee. She said she knows Mama."

CHAPTER

26

SONDRA MURPHY'S DRUG-SICKENED eyes stared out at me. I'd made it past the two lookouts, past the half-dead smoke heads in the lobby, and up the stairs to knock on her second-story door. She'd opened the door and propped her scrawny bones against the door frame, white knuckles betraying her feigned nonchalance.

"Who are you?" she asked.

"Ronnie Ventana," I said. "We talked the other day, remember?"

Not even a trace of recognition. "Are you a cop?"

"I'm a private eye. I'm looking into the murder of your father, remember?"

Her stoned-out eyes didn't even register. For a second I considered just turning around and walking away. Her brain was fried. What could she possibly tell me?

"I've got to sit down," she muttered, then loosened her grip on the doorframe and backed into the apartment, leaving the door open behind her.

I followed her into the living room. The shades were drawn, and two unkempt women were stretched out on the floor, dozing. One of them snored and shifted, but didn't wake up when we came in. The other one could have been dead for all the life she had in her.

Sondra collapsed into a tattered armchair, laid her head against the backrest, and closed her eyes.

I thought of this apartment and the house where her father had lived and wondered what path had brought her here. A lot of kids who grow up rich don't care about material stuff, but this was pretty extreme. The place was a hovel.

"I just talked to Buddy," I said, perching on the arm of a chair across from hers.

She raised her head slowly, then opened her eyes and focused them on me. Something seemed to be working inside her head, but I couldn't be sure.

Then she said, "You told me the other day you were a friend of Buddy's, didn't you?"

I nodded. "Buddy told the police today that he killed your father."

Her head fell against the backrest again, like the muscles in her neck had just shorted out or something.

"Buddy was the murder weapon," I continued. "He was duped into it."

She furrowed her brows. "What are you talking about?"

"The killer told Buddy to throw the radio in the tub with your father because your father loved music. Buddy thought he was doing the man a favor."

She rubbed her arm and glanced at the passed-out woman in the corner. She sighed and turned her dull eyes back to mine. "Well, he's gone now. Never more to scream in my face."

I couldn't believe it. I'd just told her her son, retarded and unable to look out for himself, had been set up for murder, and all she could think about was herself. I took a deep breath.

"Your father's gone, yes. But Buddy's in trouble. He needs your help."

"Mine?" She couldn't have sounded any more surprised than if I'd told her I could fly.

"Buddy told me the woman who conned him is a friend of yours."

She gave me a blank look. "What?"

I repeated what I'd just said and watched the slow light of comprehension dawn on her face. It was like she was working off the drug fog by using sheer willpower.

"Buddy's retarded," she said. "You can't believe everything he says."

"He wouldn't lie."

Again the struggle to clear her mind. "Maybe. But I don't have any reason for wanting my father dead."

"Money?"

She stared at her feet for such a long time, I thought she'd passed out. Then she said, "Good old Dad. Right. Let me tell you about good old Dad. Every couple of years he'd invite me over and give me a lecture about drugs. That's it. That's all. No money. Ever. I don't have any reason for wanting him alive, but I don't have any reason for wanting him dead either." She rubbed her arms and slumped farther into her chair, as if the effort of her statement had wiped her out. But at least her mind was tracking better now. "He's a nonissue with me. He'd rather flush money down the toilet than give it to me."

"Will you help Buddy?"

She blinked. "Me? How?"

"Make a list of the names and address of all the women you know."

She waved her hand at the two prone bodies on the floor. "That's them," she said.

Neither one could have passed herself off as Charlotte Murphy or as me. "Come on, Sondra. Somebody like you has to be popular."

Her eyes narrowed. "What are you saying?"

I realized even a junkie has her pride, so I backed off and tried again. "The last time we talked, you mentioned a woman who was asking about your dad. Tell me more about her."

"I don't remember."

"You were having a party, you said. You thought the woman was with somebody else."

She just kept shaking her head and repeating, "I don't know. I can't remember."

After ten minutes of getting nowhere, I sighed. This was like trying to teach a sea mammal to talk. "What were you doing Tuesday night?"

"I was right here. The police asked for witnesses, but I can't remember who I was with. Nobody around here likes to talk to the police, anyway. This whole thing's making everybody nervous."

I glanced down at the two bodies collapsed on the carpet in the corner. If they were any less nervous, they'd probably need a life-support machine.

"Did your father ever mention that someone had ill feelings toward him?"

"To me? He was a one-song band with me, girl. One long, ragging song. You know what that song was? 'If you want money, get off the stuff.' One song. He never figured it out. I don't want to get straight. You know why he wanted me straight? So he could unload Buddy on me. Ever since the accident he's wanted me to look after Buddy."

I couldn't help myself. "You're his mother," I said softly.

She stopped rubbing her arms and stared in the dim light at the carpet.

"Not really," she said. "Not anymore."

I sat there in silence, watching her drift. After what seemed like a full five minutes, she raised her eyes to meet mine.

"To tell you the truth, I don't know anybody who liked my father."

"Buddy did."

"Buddy likes anybody who'll talk to him. He doesn't care if they're controlling, manipulative bullies."

"Did Buddy ever mention his friend, somebody called Ronnie?"

"Buddy doesn't have any friends." She dropped her head against the back of the chair again and closed her eyes.

With a big show of patience she said, "In the last couple of months he started talking about somebody who'd drive him around town, somebody who'd take him to the zoo, buy him ice cream and pizza and candy." She opened her eyes.

"I assumed my dad put him up to it to point out all the stuff I was supposed to be doing with Buddy. So I called Dad up and told him it wasn't working. He acted really inflamed, swore he didn't know anything about it. Later he told me he talked to Buddy's doctor and she thought Buddy had just come up with an imaginary friend. She said it was normal and healthy, a way for him to cope. Buddy doesn't have any friends."

"That's where you're wrong," I said, rising. "He's got me."

On the dusky way back to my car I thought about what I had. No matter how hard I tried, I couldn't picture Sondra Murphy getting herself together enough to plan her father's murder. No way could she have pulled off anything this complicated. Buddy might trust her, but nobody else would. Nobody trusts a junkie.

And Buddy's Ronnie? Did she really know Sondra Murphy, or did she just say she did to get Buddy to talk to her? If Sondra Murphy really did know Buddy's imaginary friend, she was too brain-fried to help me find her.

Feeling like I'd hit a wall, I drove across the Golden Gate Bridge to Marin to get to my Toyota. Mitch, my ex, wasn't home. I couldn't decide if I was glad or not, so I left him a thank-you note and was back in the city an hour after I'd left it. At the Marina, I stopped at a pay phone to check my answering machine for messages. It was six-thirty.

Katherine, the clerk at the Trap and Saddle, had left two names for me, neither of which checked out when I called Myra.

The first one needed Coke-bottle lenses to see and the other one was four feet ten inches tall. My Charlotte Murphy/Ronnie friend couldn't have hidden either of those things from me.

"What happened to the retarded guy?" Myra asked.

"Buddy? They sent him back to the hospital."

"He didn't want to go there, did he?"

"No. What exactly happened? How did he end up outside?"

"I was fixing him a peanut butter and jelly sandwich in the kitchen and he must have just walked out the front door. I can't think of how else it happened."

I hung up and dialed Blackie.

"Saw the kid," he said.

"Buddy?"

"Yeah. Had to bribe my way inside. Heard you were by too. He sure wants outta that place."

I thought of his cozy room in Presidio Heights and his doting grandfather. "Can't say that I blame him."

"Doctor's a looker."

"You met Dr. Patel?"

"We got a date tonight. What do you want to know?"

Basically I told him I wanted to know everything he could find out about Buddy, about Dwight Baker, and about the good doctor herself. "After that," I said, "the night's all yours."

CHAPTER

27

"Well, well, well. If it isn't our bad girl gone good," Brigg Sturdevant said when he looked up from his papers and saw me standing at his office door Monday morning.

He was fat and oily and shaved his head. He had short limbs and a wide, frequent, gap-toothed grin. The cheap suits he wore were usually plaid and usually green, giving the impression of an unsuccessful pawnbroker instead of an officer of the court.

"What brings you down to the slums of public service, Ronnie?"

"Don't get up, Brigg," I said, stepping into his office and sliding into the chair in front of his desk.

"Let me guess," he said. "You've already been tried for Payton Murphy's murder and you're on probation." He chuckled. "Wouldn't that be sweet justice? Me as your probation officer. Ha!"

"Dwight Baker," I said, and his face fell.

"That piece of scum." He shook his bare head and shuddered.

"You've got a rapport with him, I see."

His good humor returned with a laugh. He spread his hands, sweaty palms up, and shrugged his huge shoulders. "You know me: Mister Personality."

"Edna said you'd have information on his revocation hearing."

"Yeah?"

"Which commissioner heard the case?"

Just then a small, bright-eyed woman poked her head into the office. "Hello, Ronnie! Coming back to work for us?"

"I don't think so, Nilda. It's tempting, though, with you as the new office director."

She scoffed good-naturedly at the compliment. "If you're not here for work, you must be trolling for *piñón* and *pasteles.*"

Nilda's Puerto Rican specialties were always office-party highlights.

"I'll come back, Nilda, if you promise me *piñón* every day."

Brigg patted his wide stomach. "For that I'd take on ten more cases a month."

"Bah!" she said, laughing, then dashed away to take a call from the mayor.

Brigg shook his head and smiled. "Great lady. They couldn't have picked a better person to fill the old man's shoes." He studied me a second, then asked, "Ever think seriously about coming back?"

Not a single day, not a single second. I guess the answer showed on my face.

Brigg said, "Well, if you ever get tired of free-lancing we can always use you again."

"Thanks, Brigg. About Dwight . . ."

"Oh, yeah. Let's see . . ." Brigg reached for a folder from a rack behind his desk and opened it. "He's working at Stickley Con Hospital—that's what we call it—the kitchen's full of cons."

"How'd he get the job?"

"Let's see . . . The head shrink there, Dr. Patel, offered it to him." Brigg leaned toward me. "Everybody questions her judgment for having a bunch of cons working in the same building with a bunch of innocent retarded kids, but she claims she knows what she's doing. Hell, maybe she does. About Dwight, I guess she met him and figured she liked a challenge.

"For somebody making minimum wage, he's doing really good address-wise. But that's his girl-friend's place—Cassandra Strand, society chick." He glanced sideways at me. "You knew that."

I nodded, and he continued.

"He's come out fine every time we've tested him." Brigg was talking about the drug tests a lot of parolees have to take. "I'm surprised. But he's holding steady."

"Anything between him and Dr. Patel?"

Brigg squinted at me. "The shrink? She's too smart for *his* low-life tricks. You ever meet her? She's a professional, a through-and-through pro-fessional." He shifted his bulk in the stout wooden chair and raised his eyebrow. "This tie in to Payton Murphy's murder?"

"Maybe."

"When you know for sure, let me know if Dwight's your man. He's in here every Monday and Thursday at two o'clock and I'm champing at the bit for a technicality to throw this animal back where he belongs."

"Which deputy commissioner upheld my revocation, Brigg?"

He shuffled quickly to the back of the folder and ran his finger down the page, then stopped and looked up at me, his face filled with awe. "You knew, didn't you?"

My heartbeat surged and seemed to fill my whole chest. "Payton Murphy?"

He nodded, grinning from ear to ear. "Are we going to put him away now?"

It wasn't enough to make a case, but it was a start. A foundation. A motivation. With that, and the connection to Buddy through Stickley Convalescent—never mind that Buddy denied knowing him. I'd work that out later—all I needed now was opportunity. Did Dwight Baker have the opportunity to kill Payton Murphy?

"Do me a favor, Brigg. Can you find out what Dwight Baker was doing Tuesday night? Around eleven."

Brigg's face fell. "He's in group Tuesday nights. We aren't going to get him that way. They usually go until past midnight."

"Can you check to see if he was there?"

Brigg picked up the phone and dialed. "Dr. Patel, please. Sure, I'll hold."

"Dr. Patel's his group shrink?"

Brigg nodded, then shifted his gaze to his desk as he listened to the voice on the phone. I could make out Dr. Patel's accent over the phone.

Brigg asked if Baker had been in the meeting Tuesday night. "He was? Okay. The entire meeting? Yeah? What time did it break up? Half past midnight, huh?" Brigg looked at me and made a face.

"Did he make any calls?" I whispered. Someone had to call 911.

Brigg echoed my question into the phone. "No calls, huh?" He looked at me again and raised his eyebrows. I shook my head. "Okay. Thanks, Doc."

He snorted his dissatisfaction as he replaced the receiver.

"Would she lie for him?" I asked.

"Who? Dr. Patel?"

I knew the answer before he gave it. Dr. Patel was too much of a professional and there was too much at stake for her to lie.

So who was Dwight Baker's accomplice?

CHAPTER
28

TUESDAY MORNING, EARLY, I called Blackie and grilled him on his date with Dr. Patel.

"Miranda," he said with a certain tone in his voice that told me he hadn't got to test out his theory about her couch. "She's a class act, doll, but she's got one major flaw."

"Oh?"

"Yeah. One jigger of booze and she won't shut up about herself. Two glasses a wine and you're talkin' the deluxe version that goes till two in the morning."

He'd gotten her whole life story. Harvard, Columbia, then Stanford. Founding the clinic, a couple of soured marriages, and groundbreaking research on mental retardation. Then adding *pro bono* psychiatric work for paroled prisoners.

She'd met Senator Murphy then, and it had taken her six years to convince him to turn Buddy over to her care. In the end she'd so impressed the Senator with Buddy's progress and adjustment that he changed his will to make her Buddy's legal guardian.

"That gives her a motive," I said. "She knows psychology. That means she could manipulate Buddy, maybe hypnotize him. And she's connected to Dwight Baker through the clinic and group therapy."

I heard the click of a lighter on Blackie's end of the connection, then a soft exhalation. "I'm not buyin' it, doll. She wouldn't fuck the kid over like that. Not for that lowlife."

"Are you sure?"

"As sure as anybody."

He was probably right, if for no other reason than the numbers. There were too many people involved already. Dwight Baker. Dr. Patel. And at least one third party to play Charlotte Murphy and Buddy's Ronnie. If all those people were involved, we were talking major conspiracy, and so far the only person I'd found who had anything bad to say about Payton Murphy was his messed-up, drugged-out daughter.

So we concentrated on Dwight Baker and Charlotte Murphy. We checked out three more names Katherine had phoned in without success, and Blackie and I spent two futile days tailing Baker.

He would go to work, then go out to dinner with Casa Strand. They'd go to a play or to a nightclub afterward, then go home. Both nights he was in bed by midnight. And he never once connected with anybody who could pass for my Charlotte Murphy impostor.

On Wednesday Katherine caught me at home when she called at noon.

"Were any of them your killer?" she asked.

"Not even close. Have you got anything else for me?"

"Not yet. I didn't know if I should keep looking, since one of those three could have been the right one. Will you tell me when you find her?"

"Sure. But keep looking."

"Do you want me to do anything else? I only work four days a week. I could follow somebody for you or whatever. I already went to the library and looked up Senator Murphy, so I know a lot already. I—"

"Katherine, no. All I want you to do is what I've asked you to do: Go through the store records. Anything else could be dangerous for you and could mess things up on my end. Understand?"

"Oh."

"Promise me all you'll do is look up the store information."

"If I do, will you tell what's going on?"

"Sure."

"Okay. I promise."

Later that night I left Blackie sitting outside the Curran Theatre waiting for *Sunset Boulevard* to let out, and drove over to Myra's.

An hour and a half later the box of photographs Myra had dragged out of her closet was empty, the pictures spread around me on her floor like confetti.

With her back against the couch and her legs

stretched out on the carpet in front of her, Myra ate Chee·tos out of a nearly empty family-sized bag and watched me sort through the last stack of pictures.

"I told you," she said, munching. "This is stupid."

"It's not stupid, Myra. We've ruled out all these people," I answered, tossing the last photo into the pile. "This is what detective work is all about. You keep following leads and ruling things out until you narrow it down to one possibility."

"I think I'd rather assemble watches," she said dryly, digging into the bag for another Chee·to.

I looked up and scanned the tabletops around the room. "You said you had some group photos from your clubs?"

"Can we do this later? Penelope Livingston asked me to meet her at the Paragon at midnight."

"Did I see *her* picture?"

Myra rolled her eyes. "Don't be ridiculous, Ronnie. I went to college with Penelope."

I glanced pointedly at the snapshots on the floor. "You went to college with half these people, Myra. It doesn't mean they couldn't commit murder."

"Do you really think somebody used Buddy to kill Payton Murphy?"

When I didn't answer, she said, "That's pretty slimy."

"Where are the group shots you told me about?"

Myra set the Chee·tos down, dragged herself upright, and crossed the living room to a console table with a drawer. She opened the drawer and pulled out a large yellow envelope.

"I should get an album to put all these in," she said, wading through the pictures on the floor as she brought the envelope over.

I took it, cleared a spot on the floor, and emptied the contents of the envelope on the carpet. Myra slipped back into her position against the couch and craned her neck to glimpse the top photo.

"That's the equestrian club," she said, reaching for the bag of Chee·tos. "Huntsville, we called it."

The black-and-white was full of bright-faced young women in full English riding gear: tall Van Dyke boots, white breeches, and dark, tailored jackets.

Most of their faces were obscured by the shadows cast by their smart little helmets, but a couple of the women in the front row had taken their hats off and held them at their side. Myra was one of them.

And next to her, standing tall and smiling brightly at the camera, was my Charlotte Murphy impostor.

"It's her!" I shouted.

Myra dropped the Chee·tos and scooted across the floor. "Which one?"

"Here." I laid my finger on the picture and saw that my hand was shaking. "Who is she?"

Myra frowned. "Her?"

"Yes," I whispered. "Who is she?"

"I don't know, Ronnie. I remember her, but I don't remember her name. She had trouble posting to the trot, I remember that much. And she hated the mud. She dropped out. No, maybe I'm thinking of Lucinda Rogers. Yes, Lucinda was the one who couldn't post." She pointed to a dark smudge that was supposed to be the face of Lucinda Rogers.

"I need a name, Myra."

"Let me look at it." Myra took the photograph and studied it. "I really can't say. . . . She wasn't a friend of mine. And she wasn't anybody as far as I remember. I think if she was, I would have known her name."

"Where was this picture taken?" I asked.

"Golden Gate Park. At the stables."

I let Myra study the photograph while I rifled through the rest of the group shots. This was the only one at the stables. And it was the only one with the pseudo Charlotte Murphy.

"Well?" I prompted.

"She really wasn't anybody, Ronnie. I can't tell you who she is because I don't think I ever knew."

"Who did she hang around with?"

"I don't know."

"Think, Myra. Did she arrive by herself? What kind of car did she drive? Did you ever talk to her?"

"I can't remember. This picture was taken

three years ago, Ronnie. How am I supposed to remember somebody who could barely ride who was in my equestrian club three years ago?"

"Do you still belong?"

"No. It broke up after six months."

"Who organized it?"

"Ulyssa. Ulyssa Davidson."

CHAPTER

29

HORSES WAKE UP EARLY. And I guess horse people do too. I'd managed a run and a shower and a quick cup of coffee in the car on the way over to the stables at Golden Gate Park, but it was not even seven yet when I got there. And I felt like I'd slept in.

Horses were clomping around in a paddock surrounded by stables, and people, mostly women but a couple of men, worked busily, grooming and tending their horses. A crew of Mexican men worked at sweeping and hauling hay and grain around. A couple of mixed-breed dogs ran back and forth, looking like they felt important and getting in the way.

I slogged through the mud toward the buildings, past a pair of horses tethered to metal rings on the wall, and searched for somebody who belonged.

The first person I ran into was a kid who looked about twelve. She was bent over a brown horse's hoof that she'd lifted and cradled between her knees. I'd seen guys do that on *Gunsmoke,* but I'd never seen anybody do it up close. For some reason I thought you had to be bigger to manage it.

"Hey," I said.

She looked up. Her face was freckled and her red hair was in pigtails. The flannel barn jacket she had on was worn at the elbows, and she was wearing the same kind of riding breeches the women in Myra's picture had worn. There was a little metal hooklike thing in her hand. "Yes?"

"I'm looking for Ulyssa Davidson."

"Ulyssa?" Her face crinkled up. "She hasn't worked here for ages. She went away to vet school in Pennsylvania last year."

"Anybody else that worked here three years ago?"

"I've been here five years." She laughed at the surprise in my eyes. "I'm fifteen," she said, taking one last jab at the horse's hoof, then dropping it to the ground and straightening. "What do you need?"

"Do you remember a riding club?" I pulled out Myra's group photo. She dusted her hands off on the front of her jacket before she took it.

"Some of these guys were great. I went to a few shows with them."

"Do you remember this woman?"

She peered at the image in the picture, then looked up at me. "Who are you?"

I gave her one of my cards.

"A private detective. Wow! Is this about a case?"

When I said yes, her bright blue eyes bulged with excitement.

"I'm looking for this woman here," I said, pointing at the photograph to get her back on track.

"What'd she do?"

"I need to talk to her," I said. "She's a material witness."

"What's that mean?"

"It means she might know something that could help me solve a murder."

"Murder! Wow!" She was practically quivering.

"The picture," I said.

"Oh, right. I sort of remember her. She was a really, *really* bad rider. Some people join clubs just for the prestige, and I think she was one of them. The clubs need to set some standards before they let people in. You know, some kind of test or something. Otherwise they expose the club to ridicule. I bet Ulyssa their club wouldn't last longer than a year, and it didn't. But they hung on long enough to get the clothes, the horses, and the tack, oh, and I guess this picture. Then they went on to something else." Her voice was full of scorn.

"Do you remember her name?"

"Not off the top of my head. But nobody ever cleans out the files. Let me see if we've still got the club roster in the office."

She tethered her horse, then led me into a

small building next to the stable. The wooden floor was littered with bits of grain and straw, and the sweet aroma of horses seemed fainter in here but was still pretty strong.

A huge bulletin board and miscellaneous tack hung from pegs on the walls, and a rusted set of file cabinets filled one corner of the room. A chair, a playpen, and a battered old desk filled the rest.

"Let me see," the girl said, making a beeline for the third file drawer. "I think they keep them here."

She pulled the drawer out, rummaged through the files, yanked out a folder and paged through its contents. "This it?" She handed me a sheet.

I read the heading. "Huntsville Club." Then I scanned the list for Myra's name. She was number ten. I grinned at the kid. "Good work. Can I hang on to this?"

"Keep it. We don't need it."

I headed straight to Myra's from the park, but when I got there, she was gone. I scribbled a note asking her to call me as soon as she got in, slipped it into her mailbox, and spent the rest of the morning with a photographer friend, who made me a few copies of the hunt-club picture and a couple of grainy enlargements of the woman's face.

As soon as I had those, I made copies of the list and checked my phone machine to see if Myra had called. She had.

"I'll be home for the next couple of hours," she said. "It's noon."

I drove over to her house and we went over the list. Out of thirty-nine names she identified twelve and matched them to the faces in the picture.

"Think, Myra. She's got to be one of these." I read off the remaining names for the fifth time.

Myra shook her head. "I thought I knew everybody. I guess I don't."

"Just step back from it a minute. Think about being out there riding with her. You see her on the horse, right? What are you thinking? What name comes into your head? Is it—" I glanced down at the list "—is it Martha Tinera?"

She shook her head.

"Is it Jeanne Bussell?"

I went down the list, and every time I gave her a name, Myra would stare at the picture for a while, then shake her head. Finally she said, "Jingle."

"What?"

"That's what I called her: Jingle." She pointed at the woman's wrist. "See?"

Alias Charlotte Murphy was wearing a bracelet.

"It jingled. She wore it all the time. I never saw her without it."

"Jingle."

Myra grinned and nodded. "I can't believe you made me remember," she said, looking impressed. "You're incredible."

I glanced down at all the names left on the page and at the handful of crossed-out faces in the picture. "I'd be incredible if I'd gotten you to remember her real name."

I bribed an attendant at Stickley so that I could show Buddy the blowup picture of Charlotte Murphy without running it by Dr. Patel.

We stood in the deserted supply room, bare overhead light hanging over our heads as Buddy stared at the five-by-seven I'd just handed him. His jaw hung slack as his eyes bored into the woman's face.

"Huh-uh," he finally said, shaking his head vigorously from side to side and shoving the picture back at me. "That's not Ronnie. Ronnie's beautiful."

I moved to stand beside him and held the photograph up for him to see again. "How is Ronnie different from this woman, Buddy?"

He didn't seem to understand, so I said, "Is Ronnie's hair a different color?"

"Huh-uh. She's got dark hair, but it's like yours."

"How about her eyes? Are they the same?"

"Huh-uh. Ronnie's got dark eyes, like you. And this lady's smile isn't like Ronnie's. Ronnie's nice, and I don't know if this lady is. She probably is, 'cause most people are. Is she a friend of yours, Ronnie Vee?"

"No, Buddy. I want you to look at her. Could this woman be Ronnie?"

"She's pretty, but Ronnie's prettier," he said,

then thanked me for the hundredth time for the candy bars I'd brought him.

As I left the building, I felt a pair of eyes on me. I turned to find a face looking out a ground-floor window. Dwight Baker. His eyes were full of malice. I raised my hand and waved to him like I didn't have a care in the world. Then I got in my car and left.

I did the rounds of all the local stables, showing the enlargement and asking anybody who'd listen if they'd ever seen anybody like her around. "She wore a bracelet that jingled," I'd add, but every single one of them would just shake his head, say no, and keep on doing whatever he was doing to his horse.

Stable number eight was my last bet. When they said no, I considered giving up. Then I pictured Buddy standing mystified next to me in court while Scotch Morgan barked out his accusations. I swallowed my pride, collected all my stuff, and drove down to the Hall of Justice.

CHAPTER

30

PHILLY POST TOOK the picture, studied it without comment, then looked at the list. He set both of them down on his desk and scooted them toward me.

"I'm not on this case, Ventana. I told you that."

"Somebody's trying to frame me, Post. And they're using Scotch Morgan's enthusiasm against my parents and his lack of imagination to do it."

Post's eyes were hidden behind his great furrowed brows, unreadable as always.

"This is the woman," I said, shoving the picture back toward him, then leaning across his desk and pointing. "This one right here. All we need to do is match her to one of the names left on this list."

"We? Forget it, Ventana." He pushed the picture and the list back across the desk and reached for a folder from his "in" box. He put it squarely in the path of the picture if I was going to try pushing it toward him again.

"Come on, Post. When have I ever asked you for a favor?"

"When haven't you?" he snapped.

"Listen, I'm not just trying to save my own skin here. I'm doing this for Buddy Murphy too. I'm trying to help him out."

Post scowled and fixed me with a disapproving stare. "Pulling out all the stops, aren't you, Ventana?"

When I didn't answer, he dropped his hands on his desk and sighed dramatically. "Just out of curiosity, what is it you want?"

"You've got a computer, right?"

He blinked but didn't answer.

"It's connected to the DMV, right?"

"You're a P.I. You got access to the DMV."

"I don't have access to the digitized pictures on the licenses. The driver's-license picture comes up on the police screen when you pull the I.D., right?"

He frowned and stared at the list for a few seconds. I couldn't figure out what he was doing until he said, "There's twenty-seven names here, Ventana."

"Twenty-six," I said brightly. "I forgot to cross off my cousin Myra. I know it's not her."

CHAPTER

31

"Post is sweet on you, doll," Blackie said. "That's why he did it."

We were in the Quarter Moon, picture and list spread out on the table amid beer bottles and glasses and a gray-bottomed ashtray.

Blackie drummed his fingers on the table as he studied the list. "You sure he's not shittin' you on this?"

"Lay off, Blackie. Post is helping me out. He doesn't have to, you know. I guess I just caught him on a good day."

"Better watch it, doll. He's gonna come at ya with something. And five'll get you ten, it's gonna be trying to get in your pants."

I reached for my beer. "Anybody else'd think you're jealous, Blackie."

His eyes twinkled. "Maybe I am, doll. I'd hate to lose the best friend I've got. Especially to a scum head like Post."

I drained the glass and raised it to signal Marcus that we needed another round. He replaced our empties with a pair of frosted Anchor Steams.

I glanced down at the list and read the only name that hadn't been crossed off. "Nicole Edward. Doesn't sound like a killer, does she?"

Blackie poured his beer. "What's her beef with you?"

"Your guess is as good as mine."

"She a parolee?"

"I never heard of her. And I never saw her before that day she bought me lunch at the Palace and told me she was Charlotte Murphy." I fingered the edge of my glass and stared at the blown-up photo, the one from Myra's riding club. "I just wish I could be sure this woman is Nicole Edward."

I'd matched my Charlotte Murphy's face to the name Nicole Edward because it was the only name left after we'd crossed off everybody else's. Nicole Edward didn't have a driver's license. No license, no record, no picture.

Blackie lit a cigarette and glanced around the bar. The place was starting to fill up. "Don't sweat it, doll. A lot a people don't drive."

"I'd feel better if the name rang a bell, though. Edward. . . . It doesn't mean a thing to me."

"You check her out?"

"I tried. She wasn't in the phone book, so I called Donna at the phone company and promised her a free burglar alarm if she got me the unlisted number. But she couldn't turn it up. And none of the local stables have heard of her. If she's using an alias, they don't recognize her picture. I'm going to have to go down to City Records tomorrow and start from scratch unless . . . Of course! Why didn't I think of her before?" I fished around in my pocket for some change and came up empty. "Give me a couple of dimes, Blackie."

I dumped both dimes into the pay phone at the back and dialed.

"Montague's Trap and Saddle."

"Katherine? This is Ronnie Ventana. Are you alone?"

There was a long silence.

"Katherine? Can you talk?"

"Uh—I haven't had a chance to find any more—"

"That's okay. Can you look this name up in your files? Nicole Edward. It's spelled just like it sounds. Got it?"

"I'll be right with you."

She put me on hold, and I got to listen to Beethoven's Fifth while I twiddled my thumbs and waited.

"Ronnie?" She sounded breathless.

"Yes."

"I can't find it."

"Are you sure?"

"Positive. Cedric has these alphabetized. It's not here."

I thought for a minute. Maybe Nicole Edward had married and was using her husband's last name. "Can you go through them real quick and

see if there's anybody with the first name Nicole?
Can you do that for me real fast?''

"Uh, as long as nobody comes in. I'll put you
back on hold, okay?''

Beethoven kept me hopping for the next ten
minutes until Katherine came back on.

"I found it," she said. Her voice sounded flat.
"Mrs. James Prentiss Dewitt. And next to that it
says 'Nicole.' Do you want her address?''

"Did she buy a scarf like the one we talked
about?''

"Uh." Silence. Then, "Yes. Yes, she did.''

CHAPTER 32

"Do you want to come?" I asked Blackie when we pulled up to 3329 Presidio.

He pulled out a cigarette, lit it, and settled himself behind the wheel of his hulking old Buick. "You need me, give a shout."

The door opened seconds after I knocked, like maybe they were expecting somebody. For half a heartbeat I wondered if Katherine had double-crossed me and phoned ahead. Then my eyes fell not on Nicole Edward/Charlotte Murphy but on a tiny, olive-skinned woman in a black-and-white maid's uniform.

"Yes?" Her voice was softly melodic. Filipino. She smiled.

"I'm looking for Nicole," I said. "Is she in?"

"I'm so sorry. Mr. and Mrs. Dewitt are not at home tonight."

"This is kind·of an emergency," I said. "Any idea where they went?"

"Well . . ."

She looked uncomfortable, but didn't say no. That meant she didn't want to give them up unless she had a good enough reason. I flashed my P.I. license at her and decided to give her one.

"I'm with the insurance company," I said. "This has to do with the necklace."

The housekeeper's eyes widened and her red mouth formed a perfect O. "The pearl and diamond?" she asked in a voice full of alarm.

"Right. I need to talk to her about it."

"She's wearing it tonight," the maid said.

I frowned, and her worry lines deepened.

"Is that bad?"

"Not if I catch her in time."

"Then go. Hurry!" the housekeeper urged, shooing me down the walk. "Do you know the Fairmont? That's where she is. It's a fund-raising banquet."

I jumped back into the car just as Blackie started the engine.

"Fairmont," I said.

I glanced at our clothes. I was wearing brown slacks and a sweater, and Blackie had on jeans, a plaid shirt, and steel-toed boots. "It's a fund-raiser. Think we'll pass?"

Blackie swung his old Buick around a corner and snorted. "For the help, maybe."

I grinned. "That's exactly what I had in mind."

We stopped by my car and pulled a pair of clipboards and two white lab coats out of the trunk. Lab coats work wonders for getting into places. In hospitals everybody thinks you belong if you wear

CHARGED WITH GUILT ✒ 191

one. Anyplace else they think you're either somebody important who shouldn't be questioned or
somebody so menial, you don't matter. Either way
you get past doors you normally wouldn't.

And for the Fairmont, it worked great. We went
in through the kitchen clutching the clipboards
to make us look even more important, got directions to the banquet room, and slipped in with
the waiters as they delivered the final course.

CHAPTER

33

"I DON'T SEE HER, Blackie. Do you?"

We were at the front of the room, near the dais and under a big blue-and-white banner that read, INDEPENDENCE = MIRANDA HOUSE. Underneath in smaller letters it said, MAKE THE DREAM REALITY. From what I could make out by the rest of the signs around the room, Miranda House was, or would be if they raised enough cash to build it, a group home for the mentally retarded.

My guess was they were going to make it. Every chair at every table was filled. Tuxedos and glittery gowns. Big white teeth and shining jewels.

"Nothin'," Blackie said, then raised his arm and smiled.

I looked to see who he was waving at and saw Dr. Patel coming at us from across the room.

"Blackie," she said, offering her hand and looking slightly puzzled. "What a surprise." She was so off guard, she didn't comment on the lab coat. Then she noticed me and her face fell. "Oh," she said.

"We're working the case together," I explained, hoping Scotch Morgan hadn't clued her in to the fact that I wasn't on his staff.

Looking even more baffled, Dr. Patel glanced at the elegant people around us. "Here?"

"Right." I gave Blackie a collegial nod. "Catch you in a minute, Mr. Coogan. If you'll excuse me, Dr. Patel."

She zeroed back in on Blackie for an explanation, which was what I had hoped she'd do. I went for the nearest table.

"Have you seen the DeWitts?" I asked.

Nobody had. At the next table they pointed to a gray-haired, patrician-looking man at a table in the back. My heart sank. The fiftyish matron on his left wasn't anybody I'd ever seen before. And a man sat on his right.

I crossed the room, walked up behind her, and said, "Mrs. DeWitt? Are you Nicole DeWitt?"

As she turned, she smiled at me with the best set of teeth money could buy. Then she saw the lab coat, pursed her lips, and gave me a severe look. "Yes?"

No way was she the woman who'd hired me to break into Payton Murphy's house. No way could she even have disguised herself to look like the woman in the picture. And she couldn't have passed herself off to Buddy as me either. She was twenty years older to start with. And her face was all wrong—heart-shaped with a long nose and no eyebrows.

She was staring. So was everybody else at the table.

"We're with hotel quality control," I explained. "Everything okay?"

"Well, really!" she said, waving the spoon in her jewel-laden fingers. "If you must know, ask when I'm finished. Now, please, young lady, let me enjoy my meal in peace."

She exchanged an outraged look with the patrician-looking man and turned back to her cheesecake.

Somebody nudged my arm. It was Blackie. Dr. Patel was taking a seat up on the dais. "Come on, doll. She ain't here."

He started toward the kitchen. Instead of falling in behind him, though, I swept the room with my eyes one last time. And that's when I saw her.

She was at a table to my left, about halfway across the room and she fit right in with everybody else, looking elegant but frail in a sequined blue dress, a ton of jewels around her neck, and a bright, white smile on her face. Her chestnut-colored hair was swept up just like it had been when we'd had lunch.

"Blackie!"

He turned, saw that I hadn't followed him, and retraced his steps.

"Over there," I said, pointing with my chin. "Between that bearded man and the Chinese woman. That's Charlotte Murphy."

Blackie squinted across the room. "Fuck," he said softly under his breath.

I plunged through the maze of tables, and Blackie followed. Halfway there the woman glanced up and saw me coming. I expected her to bolt like she had the other day at the bus stop, but she didn't even react. It was like she'd never seen me before.

And when I reached the table and stopped behind the man sitting across from her, she kept it up. Maybe she thought she was safe with these people.

"The police want to talk to you," I said.

The whole table went quiet. She gazed across at me, the remains of a smile still on her face.

"The police? I'm afraid I don't understand." She looked puzzled at first, then her face drained of color. Her voice tightened. "Is it Sabine? Has there been an accident?"

"Not exactly," I said.

She looked from me to Blackie and back to me again. Her eyes were full of fear, but it was the wrong kind of fear. She wasn't afraid of us. She was afraid of something else.

"Who are you?" she asked. "What's wrong?"

I stared into her panic-stricken eyes. "Don't you remember me, Mrs. Murphy?"

"Mrs. Murphy?"

It was like she'd never heard the name before. She even acted sort of relieved and almost managed a smile when she said, "I'm afraid you've made a mistake. I'm not Mrs. Murphy."

If I hadn't sat across from her for a whole hour having lunch two weeks ago, I would have bought her act. She was amazing.

"How about Nicole Edward?" I asked.

Her delicate chin dropped. All the anxiety from before rushed back into her face. "Please tell me what this is about," she pleaded.

Maybe she'd give up the act if she didn't have an audience.

"We need for you to step outside, ma'am," I said, circling the table to be closer to her in case she decided to make a run for it. "We'd like to have a word with you in private."

"Not until you explain yourself," the bearded man next to her said to me.

I glanced at him, then stopped and stared. The chair—the back of her chair—there was—something was wrong. Metal bars stuck out on either side at the back, and farther down, where her back rested, a wide canvas strip stretched between the bars. And wheels. Her chair had wheels. She was sitting in a wheelchair.

"Who are you?" she demanded in a small, frightened voice. "Harry?"

Without taking her eyes off me, she reached for the man beside her. Something jingled. She was wearing the same bracelet she'd been wearing in the photograph.

I took another step closer, and that's when I noticed she only had one arm. The right sleeve of her tunic was pinned up neatly. Empty. I stepped

back and gawked as the irrefutable impossibility
sank in. This wasn't my Charlotte Murphy. It
couldn't be. Then I stared at her face and knew
that she was.

CHAPTER
34

THE BEARDED GUY sitting next to her, the one she'd called Harry, rose and stepped between us. His tuxedo was pressed and his shirt starched. His haircut was worth at least a hundred dollars. And he was handsome: He looked like a young, bearded Robert Redford.

"You're being very rude, whoever you are," he said. "I'm afraid I'm going to have to ask you to leave."

"Come on, doll." Blackie's gravelly voice sounded far away.

"Sorry for the trouble," Blackie said, trying to pull me away. My feet wouldn't move. I couldn't stop staring.

Blackie tugged at my arm again, but I couldn't take my eyes off her.

"Please go, or I'll have to call hotel security," the man said.

"Let's go, doll." Blackie's gruff voice finally brought me back.

"I'm sorry," I said. "There must be some mistake. I'm sorry I bothered you."

I stumbled backward into Blackie, then turned and hurried past the tables and out the door.

"I don't get it," I said as soon as we reached Blackie's car.

"Maybe it was somebody else, doll."

"That was her, Blackie. You saw her. No way could I have made a mistake. She was even wearing her hair the same way. And that bracelet. I don't get it."

I stared down at my hand. "I shook hands with her. I would have noticed if her hand wasn't flesh and blood. I know I would have."

"Sure, doll."

"So why do I feel like I'm going crazy?"

"Maybe that's what they want you to think."

"Did she looked scared to you? I mean, didn't she look like she knew there was something wrong?"

"I don't know. Coulda just been somebody comin' up on her like that."

"Maybe."

Blackie turned the engine and reached for a smoke. "Where to, doll?"

"Pull around up front. When she comes out, I want to follow her home."

Blackie made a face.

"What?" I said.

"She ain't gonna walk, doll."

"Well," I said. "Maybe you're right. And maybe you're not."

CHAPTER

35

TEN MINUTES AFTER we'd parked down the block, they appeared at the hotel's entrance. The woman looked distressed and pale under the artificial light, and the man seemed concerned.

A valet brought a Cadillac around, then a huge Lincoln pulled up beside them and blocked our view. When the Lincoln pulled away, the woman was inside the Cadillac and the valet was stuffing the wheelchair into the trunk.

"Could you see her get in, Blackie?"

He gave me a hard look, grunted, then started the engine as their car pulled out of the hotel entrance.

They traveled west on California, north on Divisadero, then down Jackson. The car finally pulled into a drive midway down the block past Maple.

The house was huge with two stories, an attached garage, and large white shutters against a red brick facade. Big maples dotted the tiny front yard, and an intricate, knee-high Victorian-style iron fence surrounded it.

We stopped in front just in time to see the garage door drop. After a minute the lights on the first floor came on, but we couldn't see a thing since all the curtains were drawn. Maybe, if I got closer . . . I reached for the car door.

"Wait here, Blackie."

I hopped over the fence and scurried across the small lawn to the window closest the front door. Dew made the grass slick under my shoes. I crept between a bush and the window, cupped my hand on the glass, and listened. Nothing.

I crossed the front walk to the other side of the house and ended up circling to the back before I found another lighted window. The curtains weren't drawn completely, so I sidled up through the shrubs and peeked inside.

The room was set up like a gym but with the kind of stuff you'd see in a physical-therapy setup. There was even the same gizmo I'd worked out on when I'd broken my arm last year.

The voices were coming from the corner, where the man was helping the woman, my Charlotte Murphy impostor, off with her dress and into a pair of sweats. I should have looked away, but I couldn't because her one well-muscled arm clutched her husband's shoulder and she was *standing*. She was standing beside the empty wheelchair, balanced tentatively on frail-looking legs.

I watched, mesmerized as her husband half-carried, half-walked her to a mobile bar hanging from a chain on a track in the ceiling. She gripped it with her one hand and started forward, dragging one foot ahead of the other as she slowly crossed the room. The expression on her face was a mix of determination and pain.

She walked precariously down and back, then collapsed into her husband's arms. This was no act. It *couldn't* be.

Her husband seemed to be trying to talk her into quitting, but she pointed to another machine in the corner, and he helped her over to it. She sat and did what amounted to tiny, modified leg lifts, and then started talking. I strained to hear and managed to catch snippets of what they were saying.

I made out the woman's voice first: ". . . not like her . . . understand . . . always calls back . . ."

He shook his head. ". . . overwrought . . . has a tight schedule . . . chance . . . again tomorrow . . ."

She interrupted. "What if . . . trouble . . . call the police . . ."

"Tomorrow," the man said. He'd moved to stand next to the window, and his voice came through clearly now. "I think we should give her a few more days. She does this, you know. Remember last year?"

She answered with something I couldn't hear, and the man said, "Exactly. Maybe she's met someone. Now, I think that's enough for tonight.

Let's go to bed, darling. I'm sure we'll both feel better if we get some rest.''

She did two more repetitions while he brought the chair over to her. She slipped into it with his help, and he wheeled her out the door. The window went dark, and I was left in silence.

She could walk. But it was a heartbreaking struggle for every single inch; and the woman who had hired me had strutted into that restaurant with confidence and assurance. I couldn't explain it. I couldn't believe it.

As I came around the corner to the front yard, a car came up the street, tossing a newspaper into every other drive. The one for this house landed four feet away from me, with a familiar-sounding *wump*.

As the car accelerated, I crossed the lawn and picked it up. *The Wall Street Journal.* Through the plastic I read the name on the label: Harrington S. Wallingford. The name belonged to old San Francisco. Wallace Wallingford had founded the first department store on Union Square, built mansions in Pacific Heights for each of his sons, and left a country estate near Hillsborough that had been turned into a state park.

I dropped the paper back where I'd found it and headed back to the car.

"She can walk," I said as I slid in beside Blackie. "Sort of."

I explained what I'd seen and when I finished, Blackie said, "Fuck, doll. That ain't walkin'."

I had to agree. "They're worried about something," I said. "Or somebody. The husband's a Wallingford."

"Fuck."

Blackie blew smoke rings into the air over our heads while I sat there, gazing at the few warm yellow rectangles that were the lighted windows on the second story, thinking my own thoughts.

"Big bucks like that," Blackie said, "you can pretty much write your own card. Say she could walk, how's she connected to Murphy?"

"She was at the mental-retardation fund-raiser. Maybe they met through Buddy. Or Dr. Patel."

"Miranda's clean," Blackie said quickly.

"Clean enough to ask her about our Miss Murphy?"

Blackie shrugged. "You want, I'll run it by."

"I'll let you know."

After a moment Blackie said, "Want to try Wallingford again?"

And ask her what? I wondered. *How come you walked into that restaurant? Why aren't you who you're supposed to be? Who are you so worried about?*

I shook my head. "I need to think, Blackie."

I needed to figure out what I was missing.

CHAPTER
36

WHEN BLACKIE DROPPED me off at my apartment, it was past midnight and there were a zillion messages on my answering machine.

Phoebe Wright said they still hadn't charged Buddy, but Scotch Morgan wanted me to take a lie detector test. Then she launched into a long explanation of why I shouldn't. The machine mercifully cut her off.

Brigg Sturdevant was next. "Just thought you'd like to know Dwight Baker passed his latest chemical test again. He's clean, Ronnie. By the book. Thought you'd like to know." *Beep.*

I listened to three other calls about some old deadly boring insurance cases I'd already closed, then heard Myra's bright, clear voice.

"It's me, Ronnie. I found somebody you should talk to. She was in the Huntsville Club, okay? She remembers Jingle."

I glanced at my watch. It was after midnight. I picked up the phone and dialed, then hung up before it rang. If Myra had news, I wanted to hear it firsthand.

When I stepped out of my car and into the cool night air outside my cousin's old Victorian apartment building, the last thing I expected to see was a woman cowering in the bushes by the front door. She was hunched down on the ground, her head in quarter profile to me as I came up the walk.

From the little I could see, she looked frazzled and disheveled, her long blond hair loose and spikey in a crazy halo around her head and her gangly limbs stuffed into a crumpled, open trench coat. She was wearing boots. And a night gown.

"Myra?"

She started, then turned toward me. What I saw made me gasp. Her left eye was swollen shut, and there was an ugly, diagonal cut across her left cheek.

"Myra!"

Her lips quivered. "R-R-Ronnie!" she cried, and ran into my arms.

I held her awkwardly while she sobbed into my shoulder. We weren't demonstrative, even though we'd grown up the only two cousins in a very small family. When my parents died, Aunt Emily had insisted I live with her, but as much as I loved her and Myra and Uncle Tucker, my mother's brother, I couldn't live with them. Too many rules and too many conventions. After fourteen years of no boundaries with my parents, after losing them so suddenly, somehow I could never understand why it was important to be in bed by ten or why I should eat cauliflower.

They thought I had an attitude, but back then they called it a bad attitude. So when I ran away to my grandmother's, nobody ever came to get me.

Myra's sobs eventually subsided into soft hiccups. I patted her back and gently eased her off my shoulder. She's taller than I am, so she'd had to sort of hunch over when she was crying. Now she straightened and let her long, tapered hands sort of flutter around uselessly.

I took her by the shoulders and held her steady. "What happened to you, Myra? Are you all right?"

She wiped her eyes, wincing when she touched the swollen one, and took in a couple of deep, ragged breaths.

"What are you doing out here?"

"They . . ." She hiccuped. "Oh, Ronnie, I'm so scared."

"What happened? Who did this to you?"

Myra opened her mouth, but her eyes welled up with tears. All she managed was a weak, "H-h-he—"

She shook her head and started to cry all over again. I slipped my arm around her.

"We'd better call the police."

"No. I—I want to talk to you first. Then you tell me what to do."

"Sure, Myra." I started her toward her building's front door, but after a few steps she pulled up short.

"I'm not going back in there!"

"Why?"

"I—I just can't."

"Okay. Sure. You don't have to. Besides, I think you'd better see a doctor."

There were seven adults and three children in the emergency room at San Francisco General. They were all pretty quiet, I guess because they all felt crummy.

The nurse said it'd be a while, so I pulled Myra over to a corner, sat her down on one of those hard, orange plastic chairs with metal legs, and bought her a cup of coffee out of the vending machine down the hall.

Clutching my own coffee, I sat down next to her and said, "Start at the beginning. Tell me what happened."

Tears welled up in her eyes. I took her hand and squeezed it.

"It's okay, Myra. Nobody's going to hurt you now. You're okay. You're safe."

She nodded and took a deep breath while she stared at the floor. In a quiet, small voice, a voice I'd never heard her use before, she said, "I was asleep. I'd locked the door, but I forgot to put on the alarm. A-a-and this guy, Ronnie, h-he was in my bedroom. I was asleep one minute and the next there were hands around my neck and over my mouth. I thought I was dreaming at first. I thought it was a nightmare, but he dragged me out of bed and then—and then—" She gulped and took a deep breath— "He *hit* me. He kept saying something. I was so scared, I couldn't hear what he was saying at first. I could see his mouth and I could see he was angry, I could even hear his voice, but I couldn't hear the words. God, it was awful."

"What did he look like?"

She shook her head. "It was dark."

"Was he alone?"

"I can't remember. All I know is he hit me. Then I finally started hearing the words. It sounded like, 'Tell her to back off.' He never raised his voice. Not once. That's what was the scariest. I thought he was going to kill me."

"Did he say who was supposed to back off?" As if I had any doubt. "Did he say why?"

Myra slumped in her chair and looked dejected. "I don't know, Ronnie. I think I had my eyes closed. I was so scared, I can't remember. He talked so calm. It was a whisper, you know, one of those hoarse whispers. I swear, I'd recognize his voice a million years from now."

It didn't make sense. The person who'd murdered Payton Murphy, the person who had tried to frame me and who had conned Buddy, was a careful and cautious person. He was into games, mind games and intricate planning—he wouldn't just blast in and start beating somebody up.

"Did he take anything? Do you think he could have been a burglar?"

"My purse was on the kitchen table. There was a hundred dollars in it and he didn't touch it. He just kept saying what sounded like, 'Tell her to back off.' Then he'd hit me."

Her lip started to quiver again, so I decided to change the subject.

"Tell me about the person you found, the one you left the message about."

Myra frowned and looked blank.

"You left a message on my answering machine, remember? That's why I came over. You said you found somebody who remembered my impostor."

She was nodding by the time I finished. "Joan Brighton. I ran in to her at an Old Maids' lunch today and remembered she'd been in the Huntsville Club. She knew who I was talking about right away."

"Did anybody overhear you? Don't shake your head, Myra. Close your eyes. Think. Picture yourself talking to Joan and look around. Who else is there?"

"I don't know, Ronnie. I didn't notice." She reached up and touched her cheek gingerly. "I must look a mess."

A nurse appeared by the front desk, called out Myra's name, and motioned for her to follow.

I watched Myra disappear into an exam room, then hurried down the hall in search of a pay phone.

"How'd you get this number?" Philly Post growled. I'd called him at home.

"I'm a private detective, remember?"

"What do you want?"

"It's personal, Post. My cousin. Dwight Baker beat up my cousin to warn me off."

"Off what, Ventana? What are you talking about?"

"My cousin is sitting in the emergency room with a three-inch gash in her cheek. She's scared, Post. She's got nothing to do with any of this except she's my cousin."

"What do you want me to do?"

"Arrest him."

"I'm Homicide. I—"

"It's all related, Post. It's tied to Payton Murphy."

"How?"

"I was Baker's P.O. I violated him. And Payton Murphy upheld it."

"Got anything real to prove it was Baker tonight?"

I thought about what I had. Dwight Baker was sure to have an alibi for tonight. Myra couldn't identify anybody. It all boiled down to a hunch unless I could connect Baker and the Charlotte Murphy impostor. "Will you just please come down here?"

There was a long, weary pause followed by a long, weary, and very audible sigh. "Where are you? General?"

He was there in twenty minutes. When Myra came out with a huge bandage across her cheek,

Post was the model of tact. I'd never seen him so polite or so kind.

Myra, who'd always been tall and self-confident and ebullient, cowered in her chair like a frightened child and uttered monosyllabic answers to his questions. She acted like a zombie. It broke my heart.

"Do you have someplace safe to stay?" Post asked after he'd taken all the information.

Myra's eyes darted to me.

"We've got a place," I assured her.

"I want to call my mom," she said.

"Aunt Emily?" I couldn't keep the surprise out of my voice. Since Myra had hit puberty, neither one had gotten along with the other. But Myra didn't seem to remember that.

She said, "Will you come with me?"

The pay phone was only twenty yards away, but the three of us walked down the hall together. As soon as Myra stepped inside the booth, Post turned to me.

"She hasn't given me squat. She *thinks* it was a man. She can't say what he looks like or even what race he is. She can't remember what he was wearing. There's no way we're going to pick up anybody based on what she's given me. And what you've got isn't any better."

He glanced at Myra, who by now was sobbing uncontrollably into the telephone. When his eyes came back to mine, they were hard and accusatory. I felt my defenses rise even before he spoke.

"You shouldn't have dragged her into it," he said.

"If you had done your job, I wouldn't have."

He pressed his lips together and nodded. "Right," he said. Then he turned and walked away, down the hall and out the door.

CHAPTER

37

"THAT'S HORRIBLE!" Joan Brighton exclaimed when I told her about Myra the next morning.

After setting Myra up at Phoebe Wright's house, I'd awakened from a couple of hours' sleep feeling frayed.

Running hadn't helped. But now, sipping coffee in a café on Columbus with the sun streaming in through the big glass window, at least I was starting to feel human again.

"She's all right now, isn't she?" Joan asked.

Her perfectly styled black hair fell across her forehead and down the side of her round face in soft wisps. The red power suit she wore was accessorized: gold clip earrings, gold-tone belt, gold bangles on her wrists, and a beautiful amber scarf with golden threads in it.

"She's safe now and she's resting." I'd called Phoebe's house this morning and the housekeeper had told me Myra was still asleep.

"About Nicole Edward?"

"Oh, Nicole," she said. "She hated riding. I talked her into staying long enough to have the picture taken, then she dropped out. That's probably why Myra can't remember her. Sh was in a really bad car accident three years ago."

"Oh?"

"Yes. She lost her arm and has had about six different operations. The last one was successful and she's eventually supposed to be able to walk. But she's still in physical therapy. I guess it's a good thing she ended up marrying her doctor. Do you know Harry Wallingford?"

"We met."

"Terrific guy. He's big in the mental-retardation fund-raising area because his son from the first marriage has Down syndrome."

I asked her a bunch of other questions, trying to hit a connection between Nicole and Payton Murphy, but if there was one, Joan Brighton didn't know about it. "Can you tell me who else was there when you talked to Myra yesterday?"

Joan Brighton pursed her lips and stared at the ceiling for a second, then looked across the table at me. "Clarice Tippet and Bootsie Doledo were behind us and they're both so loud. I could barely hear Myra myself. Oh, and Casa Strand and that awful man she's seeing."

Blackie's fingers curled into a fist. "Want to roust the son of a bitch?"

"Not until I know who else is involved."

Blackie's face twitched. "Fuck."

"The whole thing's too intricate for him," I explained.

Dwight Baker was a vengeful and brutal thug without a conscience, but I really had my doubts that he would, or that he even could, think up anything as carefully laid out as Payton Murphy's murder. "Besides, we don't have any proof," I said.

"Fuck the proof. Fifty bucks says I get a confession outta him in five minutes."

"Let me talk to his girlfriend first."

Casa Strand picked up some purple flowers and started jabbing them one by one into a vase sprinkled with yellow ones. The contrast was beautiful and the effect artistic, but I couldn't help feeling uncomfortable—I hate flower shops.

The smell of flowers always makes me think of my parents' death, the night before the funeral when they'd been laid out and surrounded by mountains of flowers. I can't tell you what the flowers had looked like, but there must have been at least one of every kind in the world because I've never been able to walk through a garden, past a vase, or into a flower shop since without thinking of that awful night.

"Why should I talk to you?" Casa demanded petulantly, jabbing the last flower into place and wiping down the vase with a blue felt cloth.

Her hands were sturdy, but the rest of her was fine-boned and delicate, like a ballerina. She was uncannily like the woman Dwight Baker had almost killed. I guess he didn't want his girlfriends too big in case any of them ever decided to fight back.

Looking at Casa now, it was pretty obvious Dwight had talked to her about me. No way had I done anything to arouse such animosity in the three minutes I'd taken to reintroduce myself.

"I'm better than talking to the police," I said.

"The police?" She looked alarmed. "Dwight hasn't done anything. He's never laid a hand on me. He loves me. He's changed."

And I'm running for mayor. "That's terrific," I said. "Whose side do you think his probation officer would take if he heard Dwight beat up my cousin to threaten me?"

"Myra's hurt?"

I nodded.

"Is she all right?"

"No."

"Oh, my God," she said, then her expression hardened. "What makes you think Dwight had anything to do with it?"

"Call it a hunch," I said.

"You can't have him sent back."

"Watch me."

She crossed the room with the vase and set it on an elegant table with a few other arrangements. Each one had a tag with somebody's address on it.

She stared at the flowers for a full minute, then finally turned to face me.

"Dwight really has changed. He's a completely

different person now. You should leave him alone. Just because he made a mistake once . . .''

"Battering a woman almost to death is hardly a mistake. Rape's never been my idea of a misunderstanding."

She wheeled around to face me. "Dwight never raped anyone. That woman was sick. She wanted Dwight and he didn't want her. That's why she made it up."

"Did she make up the bruises and lacerations?"

Casa turned back to her flowers. "Some women are like that. They'll do anything to get revenge."

I leaned against the wall and folded my arms. The makeup along her temple had smudged, revealing the faint purpling of a bruise.

"I know he hits you, Casa."

She stiffened, but kept sorting the flowers.

"I know you think you deserve it. You don't. Nobody deserves to be struck."

"He's never laid a hand on me."

"And that bruise on your temple?"

Her hand instinctively touched the spot. "Oh . . . that. I bumped into a shelf by accident."

"He's got three more years of parole, Casa. If you ever want things to change, just call Brigg Sturdevant, that's his parole officer. Tell him you want to file assault charges. He'll take it from there."

Her eyes narrowed. "Dwight said that's what you want, to send him back. Well, he's not going back. He's doing everything right. He's got the job, he's not taking drugs. There's nothing he's done that will allow anybody to send him back. He loves me and I love him. We're going to make things work for him this time."

"Joan Dickerson said the same thing."

Casa frowned. "Who's Joan Dickerson?"

I picked up a flower and plucked a withered leaf off its stem.

"Don't be jealous. Most people cringe and turn away when they see Joan now. She doesn't get out much. But she used to. Back when she was dating Dwight, before he knocked her teeth out and cut up her face. She's the one he went to prison for."

Something flashed across her eyes, then her face closed up. "I think you'd better go."

I held her gaze. "Don't wait too long, Casa. The beatings, his rages, the episodes won't get better, you know."

She stared at the flowers in her hands for a long time, then looked up. "What do you want from me?" she asked.

"Has Dwight ever mentioned Payton Murphy?"

She gave me a quizzical look. "Senator Murphy? No."

"How about Buddy Murphy?"

"No. He doesn't know either one of them. What are you getting at?"

"I'm looking into the Senator's death. Dwight knows that and he's worried I'm going to uncover something. That's why he beat up Myra—so I would stop digging.

"I violated him nine years ago when I was his parole officer. He's told you that, hasn't he?"

"Of course."

"Did he mention that Payton Murphy denied his automatic appeal when he was on the Board of Prison Terms? Dwight's got an accomplice, Casa. A woman who set me and Buddy Murphy up for the Senator's murder."

"Dwight wouldn't do that. He hasn't done anything wrong. He's on parole now and he doesn't want to go back, so he's not going to do anything to jeopardize his freedom."

She gathered a bunch of flowers and took them to another table. I followed her.

"Tell me about last night."

"Last night?" She seemed annoyed and puzzled at the same time. "What about last night?"

"What did you and Dwight do?"

"Nothing."

"Can you be more specific?"

She sighed impatiently and started clipping the stems of some pink roses.

"We both got off work, right? Then we had dinner at the Cypress Club and were in bed watching the news by ten o'clock. Why is this so important?"

"What time did he leave?"

"He didn't leave. He lives with me."

She would lie for him, and we both knew it. I studied her face and wished I could read her mind.

CHAPTER

38

DR. PATEL FROWNED across the desk at me. "I know you're not with Mr. Morgan's office," she said coldly.

"Can I see Buddy anyway?" I wanted to show him a picture of Casa Strand from the society pages. With makeup and a wig, she maybe could fix herself up to resemble me.

"I don't think that would be well advised, given his condition."

"What condition? He looked fine the other day."

"He's had somewhat of a relapse." She crossed her arms and regarded me with a cool, challenging expression.

"What kind of relapse?" I was starting to think that maybe I should have brought Blackie in with me. He could have charmed her into letting me see Buddy. Instead he was out in the lobby flirting shamelessly with the nursing staff.

"I don't think I need to go into the details,"

Dr. Patel said. "Suffice it to say he's heavily medicated now, and anything he might tell you about his grandfather's death would be less than accurate. An interview really wouldn't serve any purpose."

"Why are you doping him up? He's fine without that stuff."

One elegant black eyebrow arched. "And what qualifies you to make that judgment?"

"I guess I care about Buddy. He's a good kid."

"I, too, care about him. I'm his legal guardian. And I'm his physician. There are certain conditions not obvious to the layman but which a physician is trained to detect. Buddy's seemingly normal outward appearance masks some very deep and hidden troubles I wouldn't expect you to see. He needs time to work through these emotions. He needs time free from being reminded of the tragedy that has affected every fiber of his existence."

She nodded as if to confirm her own words and folded her hands on the desk in front of her. "As his legal guardian and as his physician I can't in good conscience allow you to speak to him."

"The police—"

"The police are a different matter, Ms. Ventana."

I tried to keep from scowling. "Dr. Patel, I—"

She glanced at her watch and rose. "I'm sorry. You'll have to excuse me. My patients, you know."

* * *

In the lobby Blackie was surrounded by eager, frantically flirting nurses. When he saw me coming, he winked at the cutest one—a blond with big, brown cocker spaniel eyes and a torso like Marilyn Monroe's—and accepted a slip of paper from her, then met me at the door.

"She brush you off, doll?" he asked as we stepped outside.

I nodded, considered sending him in to talk to her later, then decided I didn't want to wait. I looked over my shoulder toward the hospital.

"How would you rate that blond nurse as far as friendship goes?"

He looked puzzled for a minute, then grinned and disappeared back inside.

Five minutes later he was back, beaming like a gold-medal trophy winner. "Fifteen B," he said.

"Access?"

"Ground floor. It's gonna be a piece of cake, doll. She's even gonna pocket his medication tonight so he'll be awake when we get there."

We started back down the walk again, heading toward the car. But before we'd taken ten steps, we heard a huge commotion behind us.

"Stop her!" somebody shouted. "Stop her! Stop her before she gets away!"

We both turned to see who was yelling. Dr. Patel was standing at the front door, pointing a long accusatory finger at me and screaming like I was a serial killer.

"What the fuck?" Blackie looked at me. He was poised to spring. "Your call, doll."

I considered what had happened the last few times I'd run. We hadn't done anything wrong. We were innocent. I shook my head. "Let's see what the good doctor wants," I said.

"You kidnapped him," Dr. Patel proclaimed.

"Who?"

"Buddy Murphy."

"Buddy's gone?" My heart sank. "When? How long has he been missing?"

"He was here for breakfast," she said, then remembered I was the accused. "You took him."

She had softened her demeanor once she'd seen Blackie was with me, but she hadn't backed down.

"I didn't take him," I said, then appealed to her reason. "If I'd kidnapped him, why would I come here and ask to see him?"

She didn't miss a beat. Looking at Blackie, her eyes filled with regret, she said, "An accomplice. You used an accomplice to take him away while you distracted me and my staff."

Exasperated, I said, "We didn't steal Buddy, Dr. Patel. And I suggest you call the police so they can start looking for him. He could be in danger."

"The police are on their way."

She forgot to mention she'd also called Scotch Morgan.

We spent the better part of an hour trying to convince him that we weren't the dastardly kidnappers Dr. Patel thought we were, but I got the feeling he wasn't open to much we had to say.

Blackie slouched in a corner of the lobby. He'd taken the high road and refused to say a word to anybody until he spoke to a lawyer. By the end of the hour I'd figured out Blackie was right.

"I want my lawyer," I said.

Scotch rolled his eyes. "Tell us where you stashed the kid and we'll cut you a deal."

"We didn't stash anybody anywhere. Just because we happened to be here when they discovered he was missing doesn't mean we took him, Mr. Morgan. We couldn't have. I was talking to Dr. Patel the whole time. And Blackie was in the lobby. Ask the nurses. Neither one of us even saw Buddy. That's why we were here. We wanted to talk to him."

"Would you be willing to take a lie detector test?" he asked. "It'll clear you if you're innocent."

"You're going to look pretty bad if Buddy turns up harmed while you're grilling us over something we didn't do. We didn't take him, Morgan. We're trying to help Buddy. We're on your side."

Scotch Morgan's pride and obstinacy cost us the rest of the day. I prayed it wouldn't cost Buddy his life.

CHAPTER

39

If I HADN'T picked up three outstanding parking tickets since Tuesday before last, I would have gotten out sooner.

Phoebe showed up, did her faithful duty, and bailed me out. My sojourns in the city jail were almost starting to feel routine.

"Where's Blackie?" I asked Phoebe, sorting through my possessions under the disdainful eye of the policewoman at the discharge desk.

"Does he really have five ex-wives?" She couldn't hide her amazement.

"Yes. What happened?"

"Scotch Morgan checked for 'outstandings' and found a warrant for fraud. The P.D. says Blackie told him that was a misunderstanding, that he and wife number five worked things out."

"That's true. Blackie sees her all the time. They're on great terms."

"Well, it's going to take a while for the bureaucracy to sort through everything. And the P.D. can't reach his ex."

"So when's he getting out?"

"It may take a while."

"Can I see him?"

"Probably not. His P.D. asked me to tell you Blackie's worried about Buddy."

I smiled wryly. That was Blackie's way of telling me to forget him and focus on finding Buddy. Not to worry.

I crammed my meager valuables into my pockets and asked about Myra.

Phoebe shrugged and walked with me down the hall. "Better. You going to check in with her?"

I looked up at the sky as we stepped outside. Darkness had set in. I tried not to think bad thoughts about Buddy, but visions of Myra's battered face kept fixing themselves in my mind. What if the same person had taken Buddy?

I shook my head. "I've got to find Buddy."

Phoebe started to object, took one look at my face, and changed her mind.

"Don't worry about your cousin," she said. "She's welcome to stay with me as long as she wants. Call me if you need anything."

After Phoebe dropped me off, I sat in my car outside Stickley Convalescent for a minute before deciding to go in. Then I realized I couldn't expect much of a welcome from Dr. Patel. I started the engine, stopped at a pay phone down the block, and found out Dr. Patel was gone for the day—probably down at the police station swearing out more warrants against me.

I hung up and called back, this time asking to speak to Blackie's nurse. Since I didn't know her name, I described her, and the receptionist put me through to a soft, girlish-sounding voice that said, "This is Francine. May I help you?"

"I'm Blackie Coogan's friend," I said, and waited for a reaction. If she was the right woman, she'd be filled with concern.

"Is he all right?" Her tone was genuine.

"He's fine." I didn't think she'd want to hear he was still in jail. "Listen, I'm trying to find Buddy. Is there any way you can get me in to see his room? It might point me in the right direction."

"Oh, gosh. I don't know. There are a few nurses who were on duty this afternoon with me. I'm afraid they'll recognize you."

I mentally sorted through what I had in the trunk of my car. "What if I wear a blond wig and a lab coat?"

"A disguise. Oh." There was a trill of excitement in her voice.

"Meet me at the front desk in five minutes, okay?"

She giggled. "What about Blackie? Will he be with you?"

"He's working another angle," I lied. "Five minutes, okay?"

She was perfect. The security person at the

door started to give me flack, so she came up, looked me straight in the eye, and asked, "Is there a problem, Dr. Holmes?"

The guard backed off and let me through. We hurried down the hall, and before I knew it, I was inside a small, sterile, cell-like room that made my heart ache for Buddy. No wonder he hated the place. He might as well have been in San Quentin.

There was a flat, unmade cot in the corner. A dresser filled with folded shirts, slacks, and underwear. The window had a padlock on it and wide mesh across it. The view was limited to a high stand of bushes fifteen feet away. The room didn't have a single decoration, not even a mirror. I turned to Nurse Francine. "He has to live here?"

She nodded grimly. "Dr. Patel thinks it discourages them from spending time in their rooms. She says it's best if they get out and socialize."

I looked around again, this time taking in each part of the room separately. The unmade bed meant he'd been resting or asleep. I opened the dresser drawers again and turned to the nurse. "Anything missing?"

"I can't tell. We have so many patients here. It's hard to keep track of their clothes."

"When was the last time you saw him?"

"Right after lunch. I ducked in here to see how he was doing. He was asleep. Or at least he looked like he was asleep. I didn't want to wake him, so I just tiptoed out."

I cast one more glance around the room. It told me nothing. Absolutely nothing.

"What about exits?" I asked, stepping back out into the hall. "What's the easiest way out of here?"

She pointed away from the direction we'd come. "Through the kitchen to the back."

We walked down the hall and through a swinging door to the cafeteria, then through a second swinging door that took us into the kitchen.

A lone, stoop-shouldered Vietnamese man— probably a college professor before he came to the States—was mopping the floor. Otherwise the huge industrial room was unoccupied. Francine greeted the Asian man by name, then led me to the back door. It had a flimsy lock on it—not even a dead bolt.

The nurse trained huge, limpid eyes on me and waited like some faithful pet.

"Anybody could have jimmied this lock," I said.

There was no sign of forced entry, but there was no need for force. A simple 'loid job—jamming a celluloid strip between door and jamb— would get you in. And if the kidnapper already worked in the kitchen, I wouldn't expect him to have to break in.

I turned to Francine. "Do you know the kitchen staff?"

"Most. Whom do you have in mind?"

"Dwight Baker."

She made a face. "He's not very nice to the patients."

"He has access to them?"

"They all do. Dwight brings them their trays sometimes. Some of our patients can't get around very well, so we have to bring them their meals and help feed them. We're not supposed to, but sometimes, when we're short-staffed, we ask the kitchen help to fill in. But Dwight seemed to hate that job, so I quit asking him to do my people."

"What exactly would he do?"

"Little things that matter a lot. Like not waiting until the patient has swallowed before giving him his next spoonful. Not wiping up the spilled food. Not ringing for a nurse if they choke. I know it's not what he was hired to do, but I've never seen anyone like that. He'd tease them and make fun of them when they didn't realize what he was doing. He's—I guess there's no other word to describe him—he's mean. I don't ask him anymore."

"Did he know Buddy?"

She nodded.

"When was the last time you saw Dwight today?"

She gazed up at the ceiling while she thought. "I don't think I saw him today. But I heard the kitchen supervisor complaining to Dr. Patel about him. He said Dwight keeps disappearing when there's hard work to do. He—the supervisor—wanted to fire Dwight, but Dr. Patel said she'd get him straightened out."

"Did she?"

"I don't know."

I stood at the open back door and studied the ground. Nothing. Concrete sidewalk, black tarmac parking lot followed by clipped lawn beyond. If Dwight took Buddy . . . If he took Buddy, then what?

Nurse Francine cleared her throat behind me. "Do you think Dwight kidnapped Buddy?"

I shrugged. She followed my gaze into the dark yard.

"What are you hoping to find?"

"I don't know. I was hoping it would find me."

I stared up at the black sky and thought I saw the flicker of a star. *Where are you, Buddy?*

CHAPTER 40

I WOULD HAVE knocked, but the door to Casa Strand's apartment was slightly ajar. I figured it was an invitation—a dangerous one, but an invitation nonetheless.

Instinct told me to leave, to go down the block and call the police, but something stronger, maybe the same urge my parents could never resist, propelled me forward.

The lights were off, so I left them that way. The door creaked ever so softly as I pushed it open with the heel of my hand. One step. I was committed. The lush carpet gave under my foot, like I was walking on a mattress.

"Casa?" I called out. "Anybody home?"

I stopped in the middle of the darkened foyer and listened. Nothing.

My eyes were almost adjusted to the darkness now, so I crossed to a doorway on the right and peeked inside. Lumps and shadows filled the room. Sofas and chairs. Tables. Lamps. Ottomans.

The curtains were drawn across the living room's large windows.

I turned and peered into another room farther down the hall. The dining room. A hulking darkness against the opposite wall turned out to be a fireplace flanked by bookcases.

My heart was in my throat. I was barely breathing, trying hard to listen, to hear the sound of another human in the house.

I passed the kitchen off the main corridor, then a bedroom, then another. The door at the very end of the hall was closed, and a dim light seeped out from the crack beneath it. Soft, friendly clucking noises came from the other side.

They didn't *sound* threatening. I glanced over my shoulder to make sure I knew where I was going to run if it turned out I needed to run, then reached for the brass knob. It felt like ice. I gripped it until it turned warm under my fingers and even then I still couldn't find the courage to turn it. By then the clucking had softened to a murmur.

I let go, backed up a step, and considered wiping off my prints and just walking out the door. I could have. I could have easily called the cops, but suddenly I felt my father's warm Mexican eyes on me.

Open it, he said. *Open the door, mija.*

So I did.

Light. Yes, light. And a bed. I was trying to take in everything at once, but I wasn't seeing a thing. *Slow down,* my mother's voice said.

Somebody was moving on the bed. I tried not to blink. Somebody was moving on the bed and smiling at me. Smiling at me and clutching a Teddy bear.

"Buddy?"

"Ronnie Vee!" He flung the stuffed toy on the floor, jumped off the bed, and started toward me, then froze halfway across the room.

"U-u-uh. R-Ronnie." He seemed to be looking right through me.

Just as something rustled behind me, it suddenly clicked into place: He'd said Ronnie. Not Ronnie *Vee*. Just Ronnie.

I wheeled around to face whoever it was, and as I turned, a soft *swish* filled the air. It sounded just like hair spray being released from the can. Before I could focus, before I could make out a face, before I could even understand what was going on, my eyes turned to flames.

I dropped to my knees, clutching and clawing at my eyes. They were wet, burning and stinging, like a thousand needles had been rammed into them. I cursed, gasping for air and weeping in pain.

Somebody shoved me against the wall. I reached out and forced my eyes open. The instant my lids came up, the pain seemed to triple. I couldn't see a thing, so I shut them tight and covered them with my hands.

My nose was running, my shoulder ached from having hit the wall, and I couldn't stop hyperventilating. I couldn't stop moaning. And I couldn't keep my fingers from clawing at my burning eyes.

"What's wrong with Ronnie Vee?" Buddy's voice sounded remote.

If anybody answered, I didn't hear. I felt suspended in time, frozen by fire.

Something brushed past me. It seemed like there was movement all around me.

"Hey," a disembodied voice said.

Buddy said something I couldn't make out. Every cell in my brain told me to cover my face and wait until it was safe, but I had to try. I turned toward where I thought I'd heard the first voice and forced my eyes open.

Everything was out of focus. Then something moved, and I heard that soft spraying sound again.

The second time was worse. I screamed, gave in to the pain, and curled up in a tight ball on the floor, clawing at my eyes again and sobbing.

And that's when I heard the shot.

CHAPTER 41

THE ACRID SMELL of gunpowder was the first thing I smelled when I came to. Then I opened my eyes, and the pain of the Mace kicked in all over again. And my head ached like there was no tomorrow. But nothing else hurt.

I lay on the floor, cheek resting mercifully on the soft wall-to-wall, and just breathed. After a while, I tried my eyes again. The darkness seemed as solid as the silence surrounding me.

I didn't know how much time had passed and I didn't know if I'd been shot and just didn't realize it or if Buddy had or . . . I blinked in the dark and felt the tiny pinpricks of a thousand needles piercing my eyes. If I could just not blink, I'd be fine. Maybe.

I raised my head, and it started to throb all over again. Then I forgot I wasn't supposed to blink and started my eyes watering some more. At least I could focus now. The room where I'd last seen Buddy was dark.

I worked myself up into a sitting position, then managed to stand. With my back propped against the wall, I took a deep breath and exhaled. I blinked and the Mace—or the residue of whatever it was—washed over my tender eyes again like hot acid. *Don't blink!*

I pushed off the wall and started through the darkness toward the front of the house. Two steps, then three. I was slowly regaining my balance. Then my foot bumped something unexpected. I swayed, reached out for the wall to steady myself, missed, and fell.

"Umph!"

My right elbow hit something solid. I reached over with my left hand and touched the lump beneath my arm. It was warm and soupy. Then I felt something sharp. I shoved my hand around some more, and my stomach twisted. It was a rib cage. My elbow was wedged into a rib cage. Somebody's *human* rib cage.

I was doing everything I could to keep from panicking or throwing up when the smell hit me: the salty smell of fresh blood.

My stomach lurched again, but I covered my mouth, rolled off the body, scrambled to my feet, and ran. I didn't stop until I was outside on the front steps. Then I bent over, hands on my knees, and vomited.

My head was spinning, my eyes were on fire, and I couldn't stop barfing my guts out in Casa Strand's front yard. Finally my stomach felt empty.

"Ugh!" I wiped my mouth with my sleeve and tried to steady myself against the light post while a million thoughts streamed through my mind: *He could still be alive. I should call an ambulance. Murder. Somebody's been murdered. Was it Buddy?* There was blood on my hands. I had to see if it was Buddy. He might still be alive.

I forced myself back up the steps to the front door and reached inside for the light switch. My eyes spasmed at the brightness and started watering all over again. It took me a full minute to focus, and when I did, I squinted at the fallen hulk at the far end of the hall.

It looked male. I could tell that much from the clothing. And he was big. But that was all I could make out. I had to get closer.

His chest, where I'd landed, was a huge, gaping red hole. My stomach lurched again. I turned away and dry-heaved a couple of times, then waited what felt like centuries for the nausea to subside.

Then I took a couple of steps forward, peered at the face, and gasped. Dwight Baker.

I stumbled backward toward the door, then heard keys jangling and the rustle of a paper sack. I turned, mouth open, eyes still misty, blinking and trying to focus. Casa Strand's tidy figure filled the doorway.

She took one perplexed look at me, then glanced past my shoulder to the prone body on the floor. I raised my hands and started forward to calm her, but her eyes widened in horror the closer I got. I glanced down at my hands and realized they were covered in blood.

"It's not what it looks like," I said. But I don't think she heard me.

Casa Strand dropped the bag of groceries, put her hands to her temples, and screamed.

CHAPTER

42

It SEEMED LIKE no time before the police arrived. Philly Post looked pained when he saw me. Then he noticed the little pool of vomit next to the front door and scowled.

"You can't stay out of trouble, can you, Ventana?" He'd already checked out the corpse, talked to Casa Strand, and given orders to the staff swarming around the place. "Come on, let's you and me take a walk."

I didn't budge. Nobody had put me in cuffs yet and they'd even let me wash the blood off my hands and arms after they'd tested me for gunpowder residue and taken pictures. But that didn't mean they didn't think I looked good for the murder.

Philly Post read my thoughts. "Come on," he said. "All we're going to do is talk."

We strolled out the front yard to a holidaylike flashing of strobe lights from half a dozen parked police cars.

"How come every time I show up for a homicide these days, Ventana, you're always there waiting for me?" Post squinted at me through the night mist. "What gives?"

The red strobes colored his leonine face pink, then gray, then pink again. As usual his expression was unreadable. But his tone had been soft; he was being nice. That made me nervous.

"Do I need a lawyer?"

"Did you whack Baker?"

"No."

"Then you don't need a lawyer."

He stopped at an empty black-and-white and propped his back against its side with his arms crossed over his thick chest. The elbows of his jacket were threadbare and the cuffs were frayed.

"Girlfriend says you did him 'cause he beat up your cousin." Post waited, watching me from under his heavy brows with all the intensity of a hungry dog eyeing a pork chop.

"She's wrong," I answered. "Did she admit Dwight Baker did that to Myra?"

He nodded. "Said you came around Stickley a couple of times, so he thought you were trying to get him fired. After you talked to her, she asked him about it. It cost her a loose tooth, but he finally admitted to it. He warned her if she ever told anybody, he'd kill her. That's usually how those losers operate."

So Myra's beating wasn't tied to Payton Murphy's murder. But Baker's death sure was. Why had he taken Buddy? What had he known or done that would get him killed?

I was just about to ask Post if I could talk to Casa Strand when a blue BMW pulled up behind the long line of black-and-whites. One of the uniformed policemen approached the car, I guess to ask it to leave, but the window came down and framed Scotch Morgan's chubby little face. He oozed belligerence.

Post followed my gaze and frowned. "Who called him?" he asked a cop who happened to be walking by.

The cop shrugged.

"I'm calling Phoebe Wright," I said.

Post pushed himself off the car and took my arm. "No you're not. We bring in the lawyers and all we've got is two idiots barking at each other. Come on, Ventana. Let's you and me have a little heart-to-heart."

We ended up locking ourselves in Post's roomy city-issued sedan. It smelled musty, sort of like dirty gym clothes. Since Post didn't seem like the athletic type, I couldn't figure out why both his office and his car smelled so, well, sporty. I looked around for a gym bag, but the car was spotless and uncluttered.

Post stretched his arms out over the top of the steering wheel and yawned loudly. "Okay, Ventana. What happened?"

"Buddy was here."

"Buddy Murphy?" His tone said he didn't want

to believe me. I couldn't figure out why, then it dawned on me.

"I don't mean *he* killed Dwight Baker," I said quickly. "Buddy wouldn't do anything like that."

"What are you saying, then?"

"I'm saying that unless we hurry, Buddy could end up like Dwight Baker."

Post dropped his hands from the steering wheel onto his knees and gave me a sidelong glance. "Where do you suggest we hurry to?"

I stared at my fingers and realized the dark ridges around my fingernails were dried blood. I tried to think.

Dwight Baker was dead. The Charlotte Murphy I'd found was too handicapped to be the Charlotte Murphy who had hired me. Sondra Murphy? Casa Strand?

"Dr. Patel's got a motive for getting rid of Buddy."

"Yeah? What?"

Maybe it was the late hour. Maybe Post hadn't gotten enough sleep the night before. Whatever it was, he was being obtuse. "Money, Post. With Buddy out of the way, she's got to be the next in line for Payton Murphy's estate."

"Guess again. Payton Murphy's will reads like this: Everything goes to his grandson, in trust with Patel as guardian. As long as she's his guardian, she gets a yearly stipend. No Buddy, no stipend. When Buddy dies, everything goes to Payton's daughter. Everything. Patel's out in the rain without galoshes. In other words, Ventana, Patel's got a motive all right, but her motive is to keep Buddy alive.''

My heart sank. Dr. Patel could have arranged Payton Murphy's murder—with Buddy and with an accomplice. But her accomplice was in a wheelchair, and now her motive was out the window. Post glanced at me sideways.

''Got any other bright ideas?''

I offered him a weak smile. ''Sondra Murphy?''

''That crack head? She hasn't got it together enough to figure out what day it is. How do you think she's going to come up with something this complex?''

''A bullet in the back isn't complex, Post. She's got access to Buddy. She can manipulate him to do anything. She knows society people. And with Buddy out of the way, she stands to inherit enough to send her and her friends on the ultimate high.''

Post stared out the front window. It had misted over, and the red strobe from the car in front of us threw sprinkles of red across the glass. He thought a minute, then shook his head.

''I'm not buying it. She's too juiced up to think straight.''

''Who, then?''

When he didn't answer, I asked, ''Am I under arrest?''

Post glanced pointedly at my hand, the one resting on the door latch, then settled himself back against the seat and said, "Tell me what went down tonight."

I did, starting with walking in the door, finding Buddy, and getting Maced—twice—then hearing the shot, coming to, and being discovered by Casa Strand.

He listened with his head back against the headrest, eyes closed. When I finished, he said, "That's it?"

"Right."

"What makes you think the kid didn't kill him?"

"I told you, he looked past me and said, 'Ronnie.'"

"The imaginary friend."

"She was there. She's not imaginary. I know—"

"How?"

"Buddy doesn't make stuff up. He doesn't lie. Dr. Patel told him Ronnie's imaginary, but Buddy doesn't even know what the word means. Besides, you've met Buddy. He'd never hurt anybody. He'd hurt himself before he'd lash out at anybody else."

"What was the kid doing here?"

"I don't know. Did Casa Strand say anything?"

"She didn't know. Said Baker called her at work and told her he wanted to stay in tonight. That's why she was hauling in the groceries."

The stuff she'd dropped when she screamed. Post was staring at me now, eyes narrowed, speculative.

"Am I under arrest?" I asked again.

"Hold on."

He flashed his headlights at the officer standing at the front door and signaled him over. As the guy approached, Post rolled down his window.

"They get any prints off the murder weapon?" he asked when the young patrolman leaned down to put his face level with Post's.

The guy shook his head. "Clean as a whistle, Lieutenant."

Post rolled his window back up, then turned to me. "You got lucky, Ventana."

I stared at him in the dim light. "Do you really think I could have killed Dwight Baker?"

He didn't meet my gaze. "After seeing what he did to your cousin . . . knowing you violated him and sent him back. There's a lot of space there for some real bad blood."

"I didn't kill anybody, Post."

He blinked. "Could have been self-defense."

"A shot in the back?" I shook my head, not bothering to hide my anger. "It wasn't self-defense. It was murder. I told you what happened. Even if I'd wanted to kill him, I didn't have a chance. Half the time I couldn't see anything and the other half I was passed out."

The corner of his mouth twitched. "I've heard tighter alibis."

"Can I go now?"

"Where are you going?"

"Home."

Post sighed dramatically, letting me know he didn't believe me.

"Just don't leave town, Ventana. Scotch Morgan will have me for breakfast if you do."

CHAPTER

43

THE HOUSE WAS DARK. Not surprising, since it was two in the morning. I rang the bell and waited, then rang again.

After about five minutes a squat teenaged boy with Down syndrome opened the door. He was wearing red plaid pajamas that matched his unruly red hair. He had a freckled face and a sweet smile, and said "Hi" like seeing me at his door at two in the morning was the most natural thing in the world.

"Is your mom home?" I asked, then heard somebody coming down the hall.

Harrington S. Wallingford, the bearded man who'd been with my fake Charlotte Murphy the other night at the fund-raiser, stormed up to the door behind the kid. He was disheveled and half asleep, wrapped in a camel cashmere robe and wearing a scowl.

"What's this about?" he demanded. "Do you know what time it is?"

Before I could answer, the boy announced, "It's a lady, Dad."

"I can see that, Sinclair." Without taking his eyes off me, Wallingford patted the boy's shoulder. "Now, go to bed. I'll see what she wants."

The boy trooped obediently away, arms swaying side to side and feet slapping the marble floor in the same determined, flat-footed gait Buddy used.

"Now, what is it?" Wallingford asked. "It's two o'clock in the morning." Then he noticed the bloodstains on my clothes and peered over my shoulder to the street. There was a hint of concern and less anger in his voice when he said, "Has there been an accident?"

I think he expected me to ask to use his phone. What I said was, "I have to talk to your wife. It's urgent."

"Nicole?" He stared, and his baffled expression turned slowly to comprehension. "You're the person who was at the fund-raiser, aren't you?"

"Mr. Wallingford—"

He drew himself up. "You cannot talk to my wife. I won't permit it. In fact if you don't leave, I'm going to call the police."

"Please," I said. "This is urgent. Somebody's life is in danger, and your wife may be the only person who can help. Please. Just give me five minutes."

He stared. "You can't expect me to believe you."

"Do you know Buddy Murphy?"

He looked incredulous. "The kidnapped boy?"

"He's in danger and your wife—"

"That's preposterous. Nicole hasn't the remotest connection to any of that. Just because our own son is disabled and goes to the same school —I only know of Buddy Murphy because we saw the report on the evening news the other day." Wallingford paused. "I thought they found him."

"He's been kidnapped again."

Something moved in the shadows behind him. I expected to see Sinclair, the retarded boy, but an older woman with gray hair and a kindly face stepped into the light.

"Mr. Wallingford? Is there anything wrong?"

"No, Mrs. Pryor. Thank you. Please go back to bed."

She lingered behind him. I said, "Please, Mr. Wallingford. Just five minutes. It could save Buddy's life."

He hesitated, pressed his lips together, then turned to the older woman and said, "Please take Ms.—"

"Ventana," I said.

"Take Ms. Ventana into the living room and wait with her, please. I'm going to get Mrs. Wallingford."

They came into the living room five minutes later, he pushing the streamlined wheelchair in front of him and she looking like a resting ballerina, well-groomed with hair combed and an expensive lace peignoir with tiny matching slippers on her useless feet. They both looked tense.

"Who are you?" Nicole Wallingford asked. Her voice was a terrified whisper.

"My name's Ronnie Ventana. I'm a private investigator and I'm a friend of Buddy Murphy's."

"We barely know the boy," she said. "He's in school with our Sinclair, but, really, I'm afraid we can't help you."

"Please—just hear me out." Neither one of them said anything, so I kept talking. "Buddy Murphy is Senator Payton Murphy's grandson. A little less than two weeks ago somebody—a woman—hired me to test Payton Murphy's burglar alarm. The same woman conned Buddy Murphy into accidentally killing his grandfather the same night I tested the alarm. Buddy didn't know what he was doing. He had no way of knowing his actions would cause his grandfather's death. It was a setup. When I got there, Payton Murphy was dead, and somebody had called the police. Buddy was in a state of shock, and the police thought I'd killed Payton Murphy."

"What does any of this have to do with us?" Wallingford asked stiffly.

"The woman who hired me told me she was Charlotte Murphy. I found out later that was Payton Murphy's wife's name and that she'd died the year before. This woman, Mrs. Wallingford, the one who hired me—she called herself Charlotte Murphy, but she looked exactly like you."

Nicole Wallingford drew in a sharp breath. Her husband glanced at her, then quickly looked away and sort of slumped into the chair beside hers. He didn't say a word.

After what seemed like forever, Nicole Wallingford finally raised her eyes to meet mine. "I'm sorry," she said. "I can't help you."

"Can't or won't?" I tried to match the softness in her voice. "Buddy's been kidnapped. Payton Murphy and another man have been murdered. If you don't help me find Buddy, he could be next."

She gazed at the lush cut flowers in the vase on the coffee table between us.

"I don't understand why you think we'd know anything about this matter," she said.

Her husband watched her in silence, a pained expression on his face.

"Mr. Wallingford?" I said, and he started.

He shook his head and looked away.

"He's just a kid," I pleaded. "He may be eighteen, but in his mind he's a child, just like your own son. Please don't abandon him."

Nicole's eyes searched the room and found the maid standing unobtrusively by the door. "Please show Ms. Ventana out, Mrs. Pryor. I'm going back to bed. Harry?"

"Please, Mrs. Wallingford."

She didn't respond, so I dug my business card out of my pocket and pressed it into her moist palm. "Call me if you change your mind. Anytime, day or night. Buddy's life depends on it."

She dropped the card onto the table next to her and refused to meet my eyes. "Harry?"

He didn't move. When she realized he hadn't, her huge brown eyes darted to his, and her upper body stiffened. "Please, Harry. I want to go to bed. Now. If you won't wheel me, then give me my cane and I'll walk myself. Mrs. Pryor, see Ms. Ventana out."

She started struggling out of her wheelchair, but Wallingford rose. "You can't do this, Nicole. I won't let you."

"Harry, don't!"

He dropped to one knee in front of her and reached for her hand. "We must. Don't you see?"

"No, Harry. Sabine isn't involved in any of this. She couldn't be."

"We don't know that, Nicole."

She refused to look at him. He said her name one more time, then straightened and crossed the room to a bureau near the door. He jerked open a drawer, pulled out a framed picture, and handed it to me.

Two women stared out at me from the picture, one in a wheelchair and one standing beside it. They were identical in every feature.

"Nicole has a sister," Wallingford said. "Sabine is her twin."

"Where—?"

"She lives near the theater district on Geary. She's an actress."

Nicole Wallingford was shaking her head. I thought she was still refusing to help, but she said, "We haven't heard from her in over a week. We're worried."

"Did you file a report with the police?"

Wallingford nodded. "Yesterday."

"Did they check out her place?"

"We haven't heard."

"Have you been over there yourselves?"

They both looked surprised at the suggestion. "We don't have a key."

I smiled. "Sometimes you don't need one."

CHAPTER

44

SABINE EDWARD'S APARTMENT building wasn't the kind to have a doorman. In fact the front door latch was broken, so we just walked into the lobby. It was three o'clock in the morning.

"It's Apartment E," Harry Wallingford said, crossing the shabby carpet toward the elevator.

I'd managed to talk Nicole into staying at home, but she wasn't hot on the idea. I needed her husband to come, though. I figured he'd add some degree of legitimacy to the break-in if we got caught.

The elevator stopped with a jerk at the third floor. We stepped into the tiny hallway, and I sniffed the air discreetly. Nothing, thank God. If there was a dead body on this floor, at least it was fresh.

Wallingford walked ahead of me and knocked on the first door to our right.

"Sabine?" he whispered, knocking again. "It's Harry, Sabine."

Nobody answered. We stood out there knocking and listening for about five minutes.

"She doesn't seem to be home," Wallingford finally said, which was my cue.

"I can work the lock if you want me to." I wanted him to buy into it before I did anything.

Wallingford looked unhappy. "Is it legal?"

He seemed concerned about what we might find inside but didn't want to come right out and say it.

I shrugged. "Do you want to wait downstairs?"

I thought he was going to take me up on the offer, but instead he took a deep breath and braced his shoulders.

"Please," he said quietly. "Let's just go inside and see if she's all right."

He wrung his hands while I worked the lock. When I opened the door, the room was dark. I reached inside and turned on the light.

The place was tiny. The living room was stuffed full of furniture. Through the door beyond, I could see a kitchen table covered with a lace tablecloth. Everything looked orderly. There was another door off the living room. Probably the bedroom.

I stepped inside and motioned for Wallingford to wait where he was. If Sabine Edward was home, she wouldn't be happy to see me. But if her brother-in-law was blocking the door, it would be a lot harder for her to vanish like she had at the bus stop in Chinatown.

I crossed the room and stuck my head into the

kitchen. It smelled of lemons and coffee. There were a few dirty dishes in the sink, but nothing looked strange or out of place. Just empty. The apartment had an abandoned feel to it, like nobody had been there for a while.

I tiptoed over to the bedroom door, reached inside, and switched on the light.

"Hey!" The shout came from a bed in the corner. It was a woman's voice, high-pitched and frightened. She raised her hands to block the light from her eyes and covered her face.

"Sabine?" I said. There was a movement behind me. I heard Wallingford's modulated voice, a mixture of relief and new concern.

"That's not Sabine."

The woman dropped her hands, sat up, and blinked at me. She looked theatrical and young, in her early twenties at most. Her face was waif-like, framed by hair cut short and dyed that horrible SOMA art-crowd black. Her skin was pale. "I'm her roommate, okay? Who are you? Jesus, what time is it?"

A pair of Klondike boots lay sideways on the floor next to a pile of black garments near the foot of her bed. In the opposite corner of the room was a second bed, empty and unmade.

"Where's Sabine?" I asked.

She gathered a blanket around her with her bare arms and swung her legs to the floor. She stared with sleepy eyes at me, then at Wallingford. "Who are you? What are you doing in my bedroom? Jesus Christ! I'm going to call the police."

She reached for the phone on the nightstand, but I said, "Wait! This is Sabine's brother-in-law, Dr. Wallingford. Sabine's sister and he are worried about her. That's why we're here."

I showed her my card and got Wallingford to show his driver's license, then she told us her name was Sonia DeVries—a stage name if ever I heard one—and that she had moved in two months ago when Sabine had asked around at the Actors Studio on Larkin.

"About Sabine?" I prompted.

"Haven't seen her in days. We've got separate phone lines but I noticed she hasn't listened to her messages. But that's no big deal." She puckered her eyebrows and looked suddenly uncertain. "Is it?"

We played back the answering machine tape and listened to three messages from Nicole and one from Harry.

"When was the last time you saw her?" I asked.

She thought for a minute, then reached for a pack of French cigarettes by the phone on the nightstand. "Monday," she finally said, lighting a cigarette and blowing the smoke into the room. I could tell she thought she looked sophisticated, but the real impression she gave was more like a kid who'd snatched one of her dad's cigarettes and was pretending to be Bette Davis or somebody. "She was going to an audition, well, not really an audition. She did some work for this person before and she was going for some follow-up."

"Did she mention a name? An address?"

She shook her head. I glanced around the room. "Does she keep an appointment book?"

"She took it with her."

"Does she have a car? Does she drive?"

"Sure. But she didn't take her car. It's still in the parking garage."

"Where?"

"Down the street and around the corner. The All-Night."

I got a description of the car, left Wallingford at the apartment, and went to check out the garage. As soon as I turned the corner onto Powell, I stopped.

Five black-and-white squad cars clustered around the garage's entrance, and a familiar fudge-brown unmarked sedan brought up the rear. Philly Post's car. A bunch of cops milled around the sidewalk in front of the garage, holding handkerchiefs to their noses while somebody stretched bright yellow police tape around the perimeter. The smell was awful, almost as awful as the sinking feeling it sent through my heart.

I held my own nose, slipped under the tape, and walked up to the nearest cop. "Philly Post around?"

"Over there." He gestured to a group huddled behind a coroner's van.

I didn't see Post right away, but as I hurried over, I picked him out of the crowd. He was standing at the back of a tan Datsun—the same color and make Sonia DeVries had told me Sabine drove. The car's trunk yawned open, and everybody seemed real interested in what was inside.

Philly Post saw me and broke away from the group to meet me halfway.

"Busy night for you, too, huh, Ventana? Let me guess: You were just taking a stroll in the neighborhood and—"

"Is it Buddy?" I asked, then realized it couldn't be. I'd seen him alive just hours ago. It takes time for decomposing flesh to get so ripe.

I glanced over at the limp, covered form they were laying out on a stretcher.

"Who is it?"

Post walked over, lifted the tarp or whatever it was covering the body, and beckoned me over. I held my breath, steeled myself, and walked up to the stretcher. I've seen worse, I told myself, but the bile rose in my throat and stayed there. I looked down.

The bloated, discolored face didn't even look human. It could have belonged to anybody. It could have been male or female. But the scarf around its neck, the scarf that had been used to strangle it, the scarf was unmistakable. It was blue and orange and yellow pastel with tiny gold letters all over it. The letters spelled SIVEN.

I pictured that same scarf draped over the shoulders of the elegant woman who'd posed as Charlotte Murphy, then stared at the mottled thing on the stretcher and had to turn away.

Post was waving a little plastic bag in front of me. He was saying something, something I couldn't hear. There was a roar in my ears. The lights overhead seemed way too harsh, and the bile just kept rising. I clutched my stomach, ran for the shelter of a parked car, and dry-heaved.

After a minute I turned around. Nobody was staring. Nobody seemed to notice. I heard somebody ask, "You know how much one of those scarves costs?"

Post was talking to a slim, white-haired man. All the other cops were scurrying around like elves on Christmas Eve. Post held something in his hand, but I couldn't make out what it was.

I came up beside him. He ignored me for a minute, then excused himself from the white-haired man and turned to me, lifting the clear plastic bag again. Inside was a driver's license. Sabine Edward's picture was on it and so was her name.

"You think that's her?" I asked, gesturing toward the body.

"We're running prints to make sure, but I'd bet the ranch on it," Post said.

"Was she wearing a bracelet? A jingly bracelet?"

He nodded.

"Shit."

"Yeah," Post said. "Shit."

"Is there an appointment diary in there?" I asked, pointing at the car. But I knew the answer before he even opened his mouth.

CHAPTER

45

By Sunday night I'd just about given up finding Buddy. He'd been missing for two days, and I'd spent every waking minute of those two days looking for him and going over everything I knew about the case. No matter what, snatching Buddy just didn't make sense. I couldn't get it to fit.

So when the phone rang at eight o'clock that night, the last voice I expected to hear was Buddy's.

"Ronnie Vee?"

"Buddy! Where are you?"

"Coit, Ronnie Vee. I'm at Coit Tower."

"Are you all right?"

"Uh-huh. Can you come get me?" Then he hung up.

I slammed down the receiver, grabbed my jacket and a pair of swimming goggles in case I ran into some more Mace, and locked the door behind me.

I could have walked up to Coit—it was close enough. I even could have run. But I drove.

After circling the dark and ominous statue of Christopher Columbus at the top twice without spotting Buddy, I drove back down and parked on Telegraph Hill Boulevard, at the base of the woodsy slope that leads up to the back of the concrete tower.

When I hit the parking lot again, this time on foot, nothing much had changed. A handful of tourists stood along the curved sidewalk, their backs to the tower, staring into the glittery night and taking in the view: the Golden Gate Bridge, Ghirardelli Square, Alcatraz and Treasure islands, and the East Bay and Marin way across the water. The happy barking of seals drifting up from the piers almost made me pause a minute myself. Seeing the bay from up here always takes my breath away. But Buddy was waiting.

I turned my back on it all and glanced up at the lighted concrete tower glowing golden in the night. Coit Tower. The place was locked up for the night, so Buddy wouldn't be inside.

I went up the stairs toward the front door anyway. There was a pay phone on the left. I didn't see Buddy, so I stepped through the square concrete arch and followed the walk around the tower to the back. Thick bushes lined the walk to my left, and on my right, through the glass, I could make out the colorful WPA murals inside.

There were darkened angled corners between the sections of glass. Anybody could hide in those shadows, so I walked slowly, keeping my distance from the wall and searching every black nook with my eyes.

I circled the tower once, then walked to the back again and stepped out onto the grass. Three big eucalyptus trees marked the border of the small clearing, one at nine o'clock, one at twelve and one at three. Between the branches the city lights glimmered like diamonds in a pool of black. I blinked into the darkness, then noticed an odd shape at the base of the twelve-o'clock tree.

"Buddy?"

Eucalyptus pods crunched under my shoes as I started across the bare spot. When I got nearer, I saw the form was too small to be Buddy. It wasn't even a person. It was a briefcase nestled in shadows that made it seem bigger. It was black with shiny gold latches that caught the moonlight and sparkled at me when I got closer.

Halfway into the clearing, I froze. Nobody would leave a perfectly good briefcase here. This was a trap. It had to be a trap. But what was I supposed to do? I looked around and felt like suddenly a million eyes were on me. Or maybe just one pair of eyes.

I reached into my pocket, slipped on my swimming goggles, and crept forward in the shadows toward the briefcase. As I got close to the far outer edge of the clearing, near the brush, I swerved away from the case and dove into the shrubs. I landed on my feet and hurtled down the hill.

There was a huge rustling behind me. Low-pitched voices cursed, then somebody shouted breathlessly, "Freeze! Police!"

I didn't stop. I ran faster, leaping over a fallen tree trunk, shoving the branches out of my face and saying a silent prayer they wouldn't catch me. It took me a second to hit Telegraph Hill Boulevard, but my car was down the hill and around a few curves. I'd never make it.

I spotted a street sign marking stairs that led down the hill, made for the opening between the buildings, and skittered down the steps two and three at a time. At the bottom of the block I turned left on Genoa to Union, then jogged down Varennes to Green, then Grant, slipped off my goggles and dumped them in somebody's trash, and kept on going.

Ten minutes later I was sitting at a table in the Quarter Moon Saloon, sipping Anchor Steam and trying hard to pretend I'd been there all night. Marcus the bartender promised he'd swear I'd been there the whole time if anybody asked, but I hadn't expected Philly Post to come sauntering in so soon.

He sat down at my table, waved Marcus away, then stared at me. "I suppose he'll swear you've been here all night."

I shrugged. "I have been."

"Come off it, Ventana. I saw you."

"Where?"

He glanced significantly at my damp forehead and said, "It's not that warm in here."

I lifted my half-filled glass. "Have a couple of these and see what you think."

He sneered, so I fixed him with my most innocent stare. "What brings you to North Beach, Lieutenant?"

"Your car's still up there."

"Parking's tight around here," I said.

Post sighed, then drew his chair in close to the table and leaned forward. "All right, Ventana. I'll go first. The kid," he began.

My heart jumped to my throat. "Did you find him?"

"We got a ransom call."

"*You* did?"

He scowled. "Dr. Patel. They wanted half a million dollars up behind Coit Tower. If you didn't make that call, what were you doing there?"

I hesitated.

"Jesus Christ, Ventana, if I was going to bust you over this, I would've brought the uniforms and Scotch Morgan. I would've nailed you for Baker back at Strand's house. You want that kid back, talk."

"I got a call about half an hour ago. It was Buddy."

He sat up. "You're sure?"

"Positive."

"What did he say?"

"He told me he was at Coit Tower and asked me to come get him."

"You're sure it was Buddy Murphy?"

"Yes."

"So who set you up? The kid—"

"Buddy wouldn't do something like this even if he was capable of working it out mentally. Somebody's trying to get me, Post. *That's* why they kidnapped Buddy."

"You're forgetting—Baker kidnapped the boy, and he's dead."

"Baker doesn't matter, don't you see? Whoever did this used him. Baker would have done anything to get even with me. They must have known or found out and used him. The whole idea was that first setup but it didn't stick, so they wanted to try again, this time with kidnapping. They're using Buddy now to get to me just like they used him to murder Payton Murphy."

Whoever was out to get me was somebody who thought I'd wronged him or her, somebody who thought Payton Murphy had wronged him even more. But who?

"Did you run fingerprints on the body in the Datsun?" I asked.

"Sabine Edward."

I thought a minute. "Okay, how about this? Sabine Edward was an actress, right? Somebody hired her to play Charlotte Murphy. She must have figured out what was going on and got killed because of it."

Post looked skeptical. "You said you saw her after the setup. She should have been dead."

"Not necessarily. I know people who don't listen to the news, who don't read papers. I was in her apartment. There wasn't a TV in there, and I didn't see any newspapers either. She could have been the kind of person who's just not tuned in to the world. She could have not found out until later."

"Maybe."

"That's why Sabine Edward's involvement didn't make any sense. It wasn't meant to. She was a free card. She was clean. Nothing connects her to me."

But the scarf. There was something about that scarf. "Do me a favor," I said.

Post groaned. "You're supposed to give me information, Ventana, not the other way around."

"It might help."

Post rolled his eyes.

"Do you want to do this or not?" I demanded.

"Let's hear it."

"Check the records at the Trap and Saddle. The salesclerk told me the guy keeps track of all the customers, their likes and habits and stuff like that. Maybe there's something there that'll tip us to the killer."

"Waste of time."

"Maybe, but what else have you got? Right now neither one of us has got any idea who's behind this."

Post glared at me, then stood. "If I find out you're holding out on me, Ventana, so help me, I'll crucify you."

CHAPTER

46

AFTER POST LEFT, I took a fresh Anchor Steam upstairs and pulled out the list I'd made when Blackie and I had gone over my violated parolees. Julius Brown. Harris Windsor. Sara Girard. Hilda Nuñez. And Dwight Baker. At the bottom of the list was the name I'd added the next day at the parole office with Edna: Joe Danner.

I wandered over to the table I use for a desk and dropped into the chair behind it. Joe Danner. He'd said he couldn't blame me. He'd told me he'd made all the choices himself and fate had dealt him the rest. He'd said he knew I wasn't the one who had violated him. And he'd thanked me for fighting to keep him out. Even tried to talk me out of resigning.

But he'd had nine years, nine hard years at San Quentin, to change his mind. He could have arranged it all from prison.

I sat there staring out my window at the lighted one across the street. The Chinese family inside was moving around—a daughter trying on a dress and her mother pinning it here and there, marking it with chalk so she'd know where to take in the seam and where to let it out. The father sat reading the paper, looking up occasionally, smiling when his wife spoke.

Seeing them so contented, framed in the golden light against the dark, I felt a burning nostalgia come over me. Maybe I wished I could have had some simple moments like that with my own parents. Or maybe, maybe I was just longing for a simpler life myself, one without suspicion and betrayal, without killing and hatred.

After a minute I picked up the phone again and dialed Edna Burrows.

"Ronnie? Do you know what time it is? Are you all right? You sound funny."

"Remember Vernon Russo?" The jerk parole officer who'd turned the whole Danner misunderstanding into a mountain. If Joe Danner was taking his revenge, Russo would be number one on his list.

"Sure, I remember him."

"Does he still work parole?"

"He had a heart attack two years after you left, Ronnie. He was on disability for about six months, then he died." There was a long pause. Edna must have been remembering that Vern Russo had made the stink over Joe Danner, because the next thing she said was, "You don't think Joe Danner has— He's not out yet, Ronnie."

"Are you sure?"

"We would have found him on the system file if he'd been released. What makes you think he's involved?"

"Dwight Baker's dead. And the timing of Payton Murphy's tenure on the BOPT puts him right in line to have heard Joe's appeal."

"I'll make some calls about it in the morning, Ronnie, but that was nine years ago. Why would Joe wait until now? Especially if he's still in prison."

"He could have escaped."

"That's possible. I know he's not out on parole."

I had only one recourse now. One path to follow.

CHAPTER

47

THE TENDERLOIN ISN'T the kind of place a woman wants to visit alone at eleven o'clock at night. Or even at one in the afternoon, for that matter. The place got its name because the cops who walked the beat in the five-block-square area that managed to harness a major part of the nastiness of the city even way back at the turn of the century got hazard pay. They got so much extra pay, they could afford to buy their families tenderloin.

Nothing's changed enough since those days to make anybody want to call the Tenderloin anything else, not even the small Vietnamese children who scamper innocently home from school every day and spend the rest of the afternoon popping in and out of the sordid buildings they call home.

The hardest of the hard core gravitate to the Tenderloin, so it was fortunate that Santiago Rosales had decided to set up his bar on Ellis Street. Not that it was really a bar. It was an exchange. People went to El Ratón Podrido for information, to make connections, to score goods and weapons. They went there for things they couldn't get anyplace else. And Santiago never turned anybody away.

The stench and the energy of the Tenderloin are unmistakable. Something about the smell of desperation always makes me sick at heart. Prisons do that to me. And jails. And the Tenderloin.

On my way from the car to El Ratón Podrido, I passed three drug deals, a pair of scraggly salt-and-pepper transvestite hookers who made me want to weep with pity, and about seven winos huddled in separate heaps along the sidewalk. With my shoulders hunched and my elbows out, I tried to make myself look big and tough, like I knew where I was going. It seemed to work. Nobody stopped me. Nobody mugged me.

I pushed open the bar's grimy black door and shoved my way into the crowded room. The stale, smoky air felt damp and smelled of spilled beer.

Some of the guys at the tables stopped to stare, sizing me up, trying to decide if I was a policewoman or an agent of some kind. But most just let me pass without even looking at me.

I reached the bar and, when the bartender ambled over, I said, "I need to see Santiago."

He raised his eyebrows and lowered his eyelids. He didn't need to say a word. It was obvious he needed to hear more before he'd consider letting me through.

"Ronnie Ventana," I said.

His surly face broke into an unexpected grin. "Ah, *sí*. 'Cisco's daughter. *Cómo no! Pase, pase. Por aquí.*"

He gestured for me to follow him, then led me through a small door at the far end of the room. The roar of the crowd vanished when he shut the door behind us with a solid, final-sounding *thud*. The door was probably not only soundproof but bulletproof as well.

The bartender led me down a dark hall to a second door, where he rapped gently and tilted his head in anticipation of the response.

He must have heard something, because he reached for the knob as a buzzer hummed and opened the door.

"*Patrón,*" he said, ushering me inside. "*Patrón, es la hija de Francisco Ventana.*"

The gray-gristle-haired fat man with a Pancho Villa mustache rose from behind the desk, beamed at me, and extended a massive slab of flesh that turned out to be his hand. "*Seguro que sí,*" he said, grinning broadly. "*¿Qué tal, Veronica? ¿Cómo le va?* How long has it been?"

We shook hands across the desk, and I was surprised at how cool and soft his palms felt. Thick black hair curled densely on the back of his hands and disappeared up the sleeve of his expensively cut silk suit.

A pair of computer terminals sat on the desk in front of him, each with a pulsing screen saver darkening whatever secrets he'd been working on before the knock on his door.

"Sit, please," he commanded.

I did. He followed suit, lowering his bulk into a chair that groaned at the load.

"The resemblance," he said, smiling and openly scrutinizing my face. "You look so much like your father. It is an amazing thing, these genetics, no?"

I shrugged. He glanced over my shoulder and nodded. Behind me I heard the door close quietly.

"Ah, yes," he said, settling deeper into his chair. "It is amazing. Now, to what do I owe this honor?"

"I need to ask a favor, Don Santiago."

"Yes." He didn't sound at all surprised.

"I need to talk to somebody at San Quentin," I said. "Tonight."

"It can be arranged. It is urgent, I take it. Otherwise why would you come at this hour, no?"

I nodded.

"His name?"

"Joe Danner."

Santiago nodded. "It can be arranged," he said again, then he stared at my face, grinned, and shook his head. "A female 'Cisco you are. Amazing. And *tan seria*, just like 'Cisco. He was always very earnest, too, you know. José Danner. Very well."

He picked up the phone and dialed, then

barked a few terse words in Spanish at the person at the other end. He covered the mouthpiece and held the phone slightly away from his ear. "They must locate him," he said.

He made small talk while we waited, asking me questions about my work, dredging up stuff about my father I'd long forgotten, like when he and my mother were arrested in Acapulco for stealing the Mexican First Lady's necklace. The police couldn't prove anything, and the necklace somehow turned up as payment for a monster shipment of rice and beans for my father's hometown of Chihuahua.

Santiago embellished his stories with stuff I never knew, stuff I was certain was part of the Ventana legend and not part of the anybody's truth except the past's.

It seemed like no time before we heard a squawk from the receiver. Santiago did something to the telephone, replaced the receiver, and the voice at the other end filled the room from a tiny speaker on the phone set.

"*Patrón,* there is no José Danner here."

"*¿Qué es esto?* No Joseph Danner?"

"No, *patrón.*"

Santiago frowned, then glanced across his desk at me. "You're sure of the name?"

"Yes. He could have escaped."

"*¿Se escapó?*"

"No, *patrón.*"

"*Bueno, entonces,* check again," he ordered,

then switched the phone transmission back to the receiver.

"They know the name of everyone who escapes," Santiago explained. "Especially those who don't get caught."

A couple of minutes later the voice came back on the line. Santiago switched him back to the speaker again.

"*Ahora,*" he said. "*¿Qué me dices ahora?*"

"He is not here, *mi patrón,* because he is dead."

My whole body went rigid. "No." I stared at the white speaker phone like it was the Oracle. "How?"

"*¿Cómo?*" barked Santiago.

"He—he hanged himself in the workshop." The voice at the other end sounded almost scared to tell us.

Santiago glanced at me, brows furrowed. "You did not expect this," he said, then barked another word at the telephone. "*Cuándo?*"

I could hear mumbling in the background, then the voice filled the room again. "Not such a long time ago, *patrón.* It happened eight months ago. He ran out of appeals, and the next day he hanged himself in the workshop."

The guy on the phone kept talking, but I had quit listening. My mind was busy picturing the last time I'd seen Joe Danner, remembering the false easy courage I'd urged on him, telling him he'd be out again soon. Back then I'd been so moved by the horror in his eyes that it had taken me months to forget. For a year I'd close my eyes at night and see that haunted look.

Now his terrified face loomed in my mind like an old, familiar ghost—a ghost I knew would haunt me as long as I lived.

Santiago was looking at me, one eyebrow raised. From the speaker phone came the hollow echoes of a long, empty corridor. I realized Santiago had asked me something. He was waiting for an answer.

"Do you have any more questions for our friend, Veronica?" he repeated softly.

"No." I didn't want to know more. I wanted him to take back what he'd just told me.

"Gracias, Miguel. Saludos a los muchachos. Hasta la próxima."

Santiago disconnected the line with the push of a button. Then he heaved his bulk out of his chair, crossed the room to a small bar against the wall, and poured two straight shots of tequila. He handed one to me and threw his back without ceremony.

After he'd swallowed, he closed his eyes and shook himself like a dog who's just come out of the water. Then he opened his eyes. They had teared up. He raised his empty glass, and, in a voice as soft as a whisper, said, "Drink, Veronica. Drink."

I felt wrapped in cotton, everything muffled. Everything except the pain in my chest. I looked down at the clear fluid in the tiny shot glass in my hand, raised it to my lips, threw my head back and swallowed. It felt like somebody'd rammed a hot spear down my throat. I gasped, choked, and sputtered. The cotton in my head ripped away.

Santiago slapped me lightly on the back and grinned. Then he poured me another one. *"El mejor,"* he said proudly. "The best tequila made."

I emptied the second glass, then set it down on his desk and stared at it. Joe Danner. Joe Danner was dead.

"I was the parole officer who sent him back," I said, looking up into Santiago's deep brown eyes and for an instant wishing they were my father's.

"I'm sorry, *mija*. But how could you have known?"

I shook my head and stood. "I've got to go, Santiago. Thanks."

I stumbled out of his office, through the bar, and out into the night. Where was the car? I couldn't remember what I'd done with it.

I started down Ellis Street, blindly rushing past all the ugliness. Dead. Joe Danner. How was I going to convince anybody that it wasn't my fault when I knew in my heart it was? He'd be alive today if he hadn't gone back.

Vernon Russo was dead. Payton Murphy was dead. That left me.

How was I going to convince the killer to respect the law? The law had corrupted, then essentially killed Joe Danner.

I stopped and looked around. Where was I? A small cluster of toughs was on the corner ahead of me. There was an alley a couple of doors down.

Was I still on Ellis? I tried to make out the street sign at the end of the block, but somebody had painted over it. I blinked and tried to get my bearings, then heard a voice.

"Ronnie Vee?"

I wheeled around. The only person on the sidewalk behind me was a transvestite, a black she/he in a sequined miniskirt and heels that would make a stilt walker jealous. I looked past her and called out, "Buddy?"

The transvestite smiled. One of her front teeth was capped in gold. "You Ronnie Vee?" she asked in a husky voice that sounded more like Gregory Peck than Marilyn Monroe.

"Who are you?"

"There's somebody down the block, honey." She pointed to the alley. "Down there. Said to tell you to come down if you want to see Buddy again."

"Was it a boy? A retarded teenager?"

"Down there," she said, pointing down the alley again.

While she watched, I started forward, taking the few steps to the mouth of the alley and squinting down into the darkness. The doors and windows were all boarded up. Garbage cans and empty crates lined the walls. A Dumpster looked like a mansion for rats and roaches, and the lone streetlamp at the opposite end of the alley was dark.

I thought of the genteel furnishings in Payton

Murphy's house and wondered how something that had started there could end up here in the Tenderloin. I turned back to the transvestite. She was still watching me.

"Was it a man or a woman?" I asked.

She pressed her lips together until I showed her a ten.

"It was too dark. I couldn't tell."

"Did the person have a kid with him? A retarded guy?"

"No, honey."

My heart sank, but just for a moment. Buddy couldn't be dead. There was no reason to kill him. He couldn't be dead. "How much did you get to deliver that message?"

"Fifty."

That meant twenty. I dug into my pocket and pulled out some more bills. "Here," I said, taking her hand and stuffing the money into it. "Go to El Ratón Podrido. Do you know where it is?"

"Sure, honey. But if you need a drink, there's three bars a lot closer than El Ratón."

"Go to El Ratón Podrido. Tell the bartender Ronnie Ventana sent you. Ask to see Santiago. Tell him where I am and tell him I need some backup."

"San Diego?"

"Santiago."

She nodded, repeated the name, and tottered off in her high heels like she had all of tonight and most of tomorrow to get there.

With the rhythmic tapping of her steps fading into the distance, I turned toward the alley and peered into the darkness. *Hang on, Buddy, wherever you are. If you're still alive, hang on.*

CHAPTER

48

THE FEET STICKING out from behind the Dumpster gave me a start, but they belonged to a slumbering wino with a bottle of booze cradled in the crook of his arm. I stepped over a discarded box of Pampers, some used Pampers, yellowed, wind-blown newspapers, and an old blender that somebody from upstairs had probably tossed out the window before boarding it up.

A paper shuffled. I froze, heart in my throat. Then I let myself breath again when a scraggly cat wandered out from behind a tattered newspaper. It stared up at me with weird yellow eyes, mewed soundlessly, then disappeared into a crevice in the wall.

I was halfway down the alley now, and my nerves were absolutely raw. My eyes burned just at the thought of being Maced again, and I cursed myself for tossing the goggles out too soon.

I took a couple more steps, realized I was hold-ing my breath again, then forced myself to breathe. The stench of the garbage at my feet wafted into my nostrils. A wave of nausea swept over me. I kept going, keeping my eyes moving, my arms loose, my legs ready to run—or to kick out in self-defense.

Where was Santiago's backup? I glanced over my shoulder. Somebody was rushing down the alley toward me. All business—good.

I turned back and crouched down against the Dumpster, keeping my eyes on the darkest part of the alley while I waited for him to catch up. Maybe I'd send him around the block so he could come up the other end of the alley. I was halfway down the alley, and there weren't many more spots left where they could hide.

The creak of shoe leather behind me told me my backup had arrived. I turned and stood, then gasped when I saw his face—or rather, didn't see his face. The man was wearing a ski mask. He was about my height, wearing a bulky fatigue jacket, baggy pants, and sturdy boots. And his eyes peered out at me like burning coals from hell. His mouth formed an ugly red gash.

"Who are you?" I asked.

"You want to see Buddy?" The voice was a ragged whisper.

"Where is he?"

He took my arm above the elbow with a gloved hand and pulled me into the middle of the alley. "Come on," he said and started back up the alley the same way he'd come.

I didn't resist. I was alive, I hadn't been Maced,

and he was taking me to Buddy. We were almost to the street when I heard voices. Spanish-speaking voices. In the next second we hit the sidewalk and collided with Santiago's backups: two men, small and Mexican, but fighters. They took one look at the ski mask, jumped my attacker, and pinned him to the ground, holding him quiet with a knife to his throat.

One of them, the blue-eyed one, looked up eagerly at me. "Want me to kill him?"

I shook my head. "Take off his mask."

The other backup reached over, but before any of us realized what was happening, the attacker slithered out from the guy's grip, jumped up, and yanked something out of his pocket.

"Mace!" I shouted, but it was too late. The air hissed. I saw my two backups clutch their faces, then drop cursing and shouting to the pavement before the stuff hit my own eyes and set them on fire.

In the darkness, amid the curses and the pain, the receding sound of footsteps echoed on the pavement, then vanished.

CHAPTER
49

SANTIAGO HIMSELF DROVE me home, vowing revenge on my attacker and tucking me gruffly under a blanket on my sofabed before he left, adjusting the door to lock behind him as he left. I slept fitfully, waking every half hour until dawn, then finally getting some real rest for a few hours until a noise at the door woke me up.

The knock was tentative. The downstairs door must not have latched. I started to move my head off the pillow, but the movement set up a drumming inside my skull that made me drop back into bed.

"Who is it?" I yelled.

"Edna."

Edna. She was going to do something for me. What was it? She was going to look something up. Was that it?

"Hold on," I said, then gritted my teeth and raised myself off the sofa bed. The room spun, but I gripped the armrest and squinted into the darkness until I felt steady. Then I stumbled the couple of steps to the door and threw it open.

"What time is it?" I asked.

"My God, Ronnie! What happened to you?"

"Mace."

The morning after the first time hadn't been this awful, and I was starting to wonder if maybe Santiago's tequila had somehow enhanced the effects of the Mace. Whatever.

"It's ten a.m.," Edna said. She set her handbag down on the table I use for a desk and boiled water on the hot plate while I dug around and found a pair of jeans to slip on under the sweatshirt I'd slept in. I ran my fingers through my hair, winced when she raised the shade, and then slumped into the hard wooden chair behind the table.

"Has Buddy turned up?" I asked. The news would have carried it if he had, and Edna was a news junkie.

"No," she answered, setting a cup of instant coffee on the table in front of me. "Here. Drink this. You'll feel better."

I blinked, then sniffed the various chemical aromas of the coffee and drank it anyway. Then I squinted across at Edna, who had her own mug of coffee on her lap as she sat in the one armchair I own. Her face was solemn.

"Drink," she said.

I did, knowing she wouldn't tell me what was on her mind until I at least pretended to take a sip.

"I have something to tell you, Ronnie. Bad news."

"Not Buddy—"

"No. I'm afraid it's Joe Danner. I made the inquiries you asked me to. The news is not good, Ronnie. He took his own life eight months ago."

The dark pain washed into my heart all over again. Joe Danner had been an innocent man caught up in a tangled web of evil and misfortune simply because he refused to relinquish his rights. Instead of respecting his honor, the system had thrown him into an abyss he'd never managed to get out of. And somehow I hadn't been able to do a thing about it. I did nothing. Nothing except suspect him of something far worse than anything he'd ever done.

"I'm sorry," Edna said. And she knew enough to say nothing more.

We just sat there, the two of us, sipping our instant coffee and thinking our own thoughts until the downstairs buzzer sounded. I covered my ears, took a deep breath, and nodded when Edna asked if she should buzz whoever it was up.

When she opened the door, Philly Post filled the frame. He was frowning, looking ominous and sour, clutching a fat manila envelope in his left hand. Edna glanced over her shoulder at me.

"He's okay," I said, then introduced them when Post stepped inside.

Edna reached for her handbag and turned to the open door. "I've got to get back to the office, Ronnie. Lieutenant, it was a pleasure."

Once she was gone, Post sauntered over to the table and slapped the envelope down. "Want to tell me about last night?"

I glanced at the envelope. "What's that?"

"Montague's Trap and Saddle." He lasered his eyes into me. "Last night, Ventana."

"I had a run-in with a mugger."

He put both hands on the table, on either side of the envelope, and leaned across it until his face was inches from mine. "The only thing between you and Scotch Morgan throwing you in jail is me, Ventana. I've been screwing around in the dark long enough. Now, stop jamming me up. Tell me what went down, or I'm giving you over to Morgan. Now."

He seemed serious, so I told him about my hunch on Joe Danner. It wasn't like I was giving anything away.

"And I couldn't have told you about it because I didn't think of it until after you'd gone. I wasn't sure it would pan into anything. What about this?" I asked, indicating the packet on the table. "Anything worthwhile in here?"

I reached for the envelope but Post slapped his hand down on it to keep me from looking inside. "I want you to go over this shit here, now, in front of me. And if you see anything—any little thing— that points to something, you tell me, or you're dead. I'm going to find that kid and the killer, and if you get in the way, you're as good as pushing a broom for a living for the rest of your life. Got that, Ventana?"

I guess that's why at the end of an hour and a half, after reading through every single record in the pack, I didn't tell him my own theory on why Sabine Edward's name was missing—I hate being threatened.

CHAPTER
50

CEDRIC STARED DOWN his regally aquiline nose at me like I was some kind of virus.

"You!" he exclaimed when I reminded him who I was. "Do you honestly believe I'm going to talk to you after everything you've done?"

"This may come as a big surprise, Cedric, but I don't want to talk to you. Is Katherine around?"

He waved his tapered hands in the air and rolled his eyes. I thought he was having a seizure, but he stopped after a few seconds and said, "That wretched girl."

"What did she do?" I asked.

He glanced at the shop door to make sure nobody was coming, then dropped his voice to a stage whisper. "I had to let her go."

"Why?"

"Theft. She stole a Siven scarf."

"One of the blue-and-orange pastels?"

Cedric's eyes narrowed. "How did you know?"

"Call it an unlucky guess."

* * *

On my way over to Nicole Wallingford's house I stopped by a pay phone to check for messages. Phoebe had phoned asking if I'd heard anything from Buddy and would I please check in with her because the court had asked where I was.

The second call was from Myra. She sounded not quite like her old self but better. She was back home and wanted to know if I'd found Buddy yet. And would I please set aside some time to come over and beef up her burglar alarm system?

The last message was from Blackie. "I'm out, doll. I'll be at the Moon at noon."

I checked my watch. A quarter till. Nicole Wallingford would have to wait. I dropped two coins into the phone and dialed.

"Edna?"

"Ronnie. Are you doing okay?"

"Did you check to see which commissioner sent Danner back?"

"Yes."

"Payton Murphy?"

"Yes. Does that make sense?"

"That's one way of putting it."

"Are you all right?"

"I've been better. Thanks, Edna."

Blackie was strolling on the sidewalk on his way to the Quarter Moon Saloon's front door when I slowed the car down and honked. He'd been home already, I could tell, because he was clean shaven and had changed his clothes.

"Hey, jailbird," I said when he climbed in beside me.

"Find the kid yet?" he asked.

I put the car in gear and drove. "No, but I know who's got him."

"Who?"

"Joe Danner's sister."

"Danner? The reporter you been beatin' yourself over the head with all this time? Fuck."

"He killed himself eight months ago."

"That's too bad, doll. I know you had a lot a respect for the guy." He reached inside his shirt pocket for a smoke. "Kid sister's blaming you and Murphy?"

I nodded.

"How's Buddy fit?"

"He's just a means to an end."

Blackie's usually sexy blue eyes hardened. "You know where she lives?"

I nodded.

"Fuck. Let's go get her."

"No. That way's too dangerous. If we surprise her like that, she could kill Buddy before we get to him. No. She's coming to us, Blackie. And she's going to tell us exactly where she's stashed Buddy."

"Yeah? How?"

Nicole Wallingford's delicate face was drawn. Her clothes were perfectly pressed and tailored, but her skin was colorless and her big doe eyes were rimmed in red. I'd spent the last hour circling the city and driving erratically trying to lose the S.F.P.D. tail I'd noticed this morning. She'd been good but not good enough. I'd finally dropped her at Market and Third and made the meet with fifteen minutes to spare.

Harry Wallingford stood behind Nicole, his hand resting protectively on her thin shoulder.

"Can't you do this without Nicole?" he asked.

I'd tried to come up with a way to exclude her but if I was going to negotiate for Buddy's whereabouts, I needed a pretty big chip to throw into the pot. Trading "Sabine's" silence would only work if I could prove Sabine was still alive. I started to explain all this again to Harry, but Nicole's narrow fingers found his and held them until her knuckles turned white.

"No, Harry. I want to help. Please." She turned to me. "Tell me what I have to do."

"I'll make the call," I said. "Then you sit at the table so she can see you."

"Will she be in any danger?" Wallingford asked.

"Blackie'll be right next to her," I said. "If Katherine tries anything, Blackie will handle it."

Wallingford seemed reassured when he glanced at Blackie, who was standing next to me, absently clenching and unclenching his fists. In spite of his grizzled hair Blackie looked tough enough to take on a platoon.

"If she has a gun?" Wallingford asked.

"I'll take the bullet," Blackie said.

Nicole looked both alarmed and impressed. "You'd do that for Buddy?"

Blackie's jaw tightened. "You got a beef with somebody, you don't bring kids into it," he said.

The call went just like I'd planned. I left Nicole and Harry Wallingford and Blackie sitting grimly at a table in the back of the bar and went into Santiago's office. I made my voice sound raspy enough to make somebody buy the possibility that I'd been strangled and left for dead.

"You should have made sure I was dead," I began when she picked up the phone.

"Who is this?"

"Who else have you strangled lately?"

"Who is this?"

"Next time make sure your victim's dead. You're going to have to pay now. Meet me at El Ratón Podrido on Ellis in half an hour and we'll discuss terms. Believe me, it's going to cost you more than a scarf this time. And don't try anything. I've got a bodyguard."

"Why sh—"

"Be there, or I'm going to the police." I slammed the receiver down and looked up into Santiago's beaming face.

"Excellent!" he proclaimed. "Your *padre*, he would have been proud. Now let's go tell my patrons what they're in for tonight."

CHAPTER

51

THE WOMAN WALKED in first. I was at a little table by the door with my back to her, but I could see her reflection in the mirror over the bar.

She didn't look at all like the person I'd seen at Montague's Trap and Saddle. She wore a dark wig cut to my style and dark makeup that matched my complexion. No wonder Buddy had described me when he described the woman who'd tricked him into killing his grandfather.

The man who walked in behind her was as tall as Buddy and built like him, but he had a determined gait instead of Buddy's flat-footed, easy step. He greeted one of the men at the bar, then crossed the room to settle onto the stool next to him. He was one of the regulars, not connected to the woman who now stood alone at the door.

I prayed Buddy would come through the door next, but I knew he wouldn't. Was he still alive? I glanced at her, and my heart sank. She was wired, a fever in her eyes and a jittery air about her that told me she was ready to snap. She looked capable of anything.

I craned my neck as unobtrusively as I could, trying to locate her hands. The left one was visible, clenching and unclenching at her side, but the other one was buried in her pocket.

The tiny band of Santiago's customers who'd decided to stay for the rumble played their parts well. Two looked her over, and the other three pretended to ignore her. Santiago, who'd donned a white apron and joined the bartender behind the bar, seemed the picture of ease, telling stories and getting the men to laugh without ever taking his eyes off her.

She stared back at them all, scanning the room with a defiant self-confidence that told me she had a gun.

We'd talked Harry into sitting out of sight behind one of the fat guys at the bar, but Nicole was at a table with Blackie in the back of the room. A coat hung over the back of her wheelchair and she sat with a jacket draped over her shoulders to hide her missing right arm. Just the same, in El Ratón Podrido, with the pastel Siven scarf we'd borrowed from Cedric, she stood out like a lily in a swamp.

As soon as Katherine's gaze fell on her, Nicole's eyes took on a deer-in-the-headlights glaze that told me we were in trouble.

Katherine stiffened, then, from where she

stood, with her hand still in her pocket, raised the gun toward Nicole.

"She's gonna shoot!" somebody yelled.

Blackie threw himself over Nicole just as four quick shots ripped through the air. Harry flung himself toward his wife.

"She's getting away!" Santiago shouted, pointing.

I turned in time to see Katherine vanish out the door. In the rush to get out I knocked my chair over and tripped. But I was still the first one to hit the sidewalk.

The man we'd posted outside was on the ground, cursing and rubbing his eyes. Mace. I looked around, but the street was deserted. There was no sign of her except for the hollow echo of running footsteps in the distance. I ran down the street toward the sound, then caught a flash of movement down an alley to the right. I took off running and ignored the shout to wait from behind me.

I saw her shadow vanish again ahead of me as she turned another corner at the far end of the alley. I doubled my speed and flew past empty boxes and beer bottles and big dark things that blocked doorways.

Three blocks, four. Then five. We were in the very bowels of the Tenderloin now. I'd glanced back once to see if anybody was even close to catching up with us, but the street was deserted. I'd left everybody else behind, and I was gaining on her. She had fear on her side, but I had years and miles of running.

One more block and I was close enough to hear her ragged panting, to see the gun in her hand. Suddenly she slowed, then stopped and turned, raising the gun. A shot rang out, and a window shattered behind me. She was too winded to shoot straight.

Before she could get into position to fire again, I closed the distance between us and hurled myself right into her. She fell to the pavement, and the gun skittered across the wet asphalt. I kicked it under a Dumpster a few feet away, then turned to find Katherine struggling to her feet.

As soon as she was upright, she tilted her quivering right hand so that a glint of metal caught the light from the streetlamp. It wasn't a gun but it was something just as effective: Mace.

"Don't move!" she shouted breathlessly. "Get back! Against the wall."

I eased myself over slowly until my back touched the wall. My breath was coming in jagged gasps.

"You should have stayed in jail," Katherine hissed. "Now I'm going to have to kill you."

She sidled up to the Dumpster, trying to catch her breath and, holding the Mace, reached under it for the gun. For a split second I considered rushing her, but the notion of being blinded again held me in check.

"I thought you'd remember me," Katherine

said. "That's why I hired that actress—because I was afraid you'd recognize me. Then you walked right into the store and didn't even know who I was."

"It's not too late to stop all this," I said.

"Yes, it is," she said. "It's far too late."

"You don't have to go on with this. I'm sure the D.A. will go easy on you if you just tell us where Buddy is."

"Easy? *Easy*? Like they did Joe?" She tilted her head into the light, and I saw her eyes. They were filled with such hate they barely seemed human. The wig was gone now, and her blond hair was disheveled. Her clothes were torn, but in that faintest of lights I saw the resemblance to the little girl I'd known nine years ago.

She'd been twelve that last time I'd seen her, the last time I'd made a home visit to check on Joe Danner. That had been before he'd been violated, before he'd been sent back. She'd been a skinny little girl with a ponytail. A scrawny kid who adored her big brother, the reporter.

"Joe didn't commit that first murder," she growled. "They framed him to try to get him to talk. They thought they could break him, but he wouldn't give them the satisfaction. He did his time, his four years, and then he was ready to live, to leave all that behind and get on with his life. It takes a pretty big man to do something like that— to serve time when you know you're innocent. But he was ready to forget about it, to forget those lost years, to put it all behind him and go on with life. Until *you* sent him back.''

I stood frozen against the wall, listening and watching for an opening. I wondered if anybody in the neighborhood would actually call the police if they heard a gunshot.

''Put the gun down, Katherine. We can talk, and everything will be all right. Just tell me if Buddy's all right.''

''All right? What do you care about Buddy?''

''He's innocent,'' I said before I realized what I was saying.

''So was Joe! Why didn't you care about him?''

''I did.''

''Is that why you sent him back? You're so concerned about Buddy, but you couldn't lift a finger for Joe. Not that second time. You just let him rot.''

''That's not true, Katherine. I—''

''Why didn't you care about *him*?''

''I did. Katherine, it's not . . .'' There was too much to explain. I spread my arms and sort of shrugged.

''You sent him back to that hell.''

''I didn't want to.''

''But you did. Just like Payton Murphy did. And now you're going to pay, just like Payton Murphy paid.''

''Do you think this is what Joe would want you to do? Is this how you want to honor his memory?''

She took another step closer and raised the

gun. "His memory? *His memory?* Let me tell you about his memory, the part that will live forever in my mind. My memory is watching Joe die a little bit every day, bit by bit, lost appeal by lost appeal. Every week when I went to visit him, I could see him slipping away. My mother saw it too. That's what killed her. My God, it's killed me. Except for the hate, I'm dead inside."

Her eyes were crazy, filled with the wildness of vengeance. "I wanted you to go to jail," she said, "and think about what it was like to be there when you're innocent, when you've been framed like Joe was."

"Why use Buddy?"

Her hand, the one holding the gun, dropped a few inches. "It was the only way I could think to get to Payton Murphy. When I first thought of making friends with Buddy, I was going to kill Buddy. I knew Murphy loved Buddy more than his own life. Then I came up with a better plan— kill Murphy and frame you all at the same—"

Just then the transvestite with the Gregory Peck voice stumbled around the corner behind Katherine. She was in a red-sequined sheath with matching shoes and a plumed hat that would have looked great on Myrna Loy.

"Excuse me, honey," she said in her deep, gravelly voice, "but don't you know that's illegal."

Katherine turned, startled, toward the intruder. It was all I needed.

I lunged for her arm and knocked her to the ground just as I heard voices shouting behind the transvestite. Two men, short Mexicans from El Ratón, ran toward us, shouting in Spanish.

"*¡Allí! Mira.*"

"*¡La rubia!*"

Katherine fell in a heap under me while the two backups swarmed on either side of us, one taking her arms and the other spotting the gun under the Dumpster beside us. They were the same two who had helped me out the other night.

"Where's Buddy?" I demanded, breathing hard and leaning in toward her as I pinned her shoulders to the ground. "Tell me what you did with him."

She pursed her lips and spat in my face.

"*¡Coño!*" said the Mexican behind me. The other one was still holding Katherine's arms over her head.

"YOU KILLED HIM!" she screamed over and over again. "YOU KILLED HIM!"

She didn't stop until she saw the tears in my eyes. Then she turned her face away and sobbed.

"Nothing we can do will ever bring him back, Katherine. I'm sorry."

I rose and motioned for the guys to bring her to her feet. She stood, head low, sobbing quietly.

"Where's Buddy?" I asked again.

She kept her head down, shook it, and kept on crying.

"Is he at your place?"

She didn't answer. I searched her pockets until I found a wallet. The address was out in the Avenues, in the Richmond, her mother's house, the same house where I'd made home visits to her brother when he was on parole.

"Come on. Let's take a ride," I said, and prayed she'd used up all her imagination dreaming of ways to put me in jail.

As SOON AS we turned off Balboa onto Thirty-second and stopped in front of Katherine's house, my heart sank. The front door gaped wide open and the lights from inside blazed into the night. The street was deserted.

"¿Y ahora qué?" one of Santiago's guys in the backseat asked.

He sounded as unhappy as I felt. His companion said very clearly, in English, "No cops."

On the way to the car I'd asked about Blackie, and they'd told me through signs and words that he'd been hit. But it wasn't "serio." He'd even started out running with them after me, but hadn't been able to keep up.

Police cars covered the block in front of the bar, so I hadn't stopped.

Now, parked across the street from Katherine's house, I undid my belt buckle and tossed the belt over the backseat to them. "Tie her up," I said. "Then you can go. All right?"

They twisted her around for me to see how they'd secured her hands.

"Okay. Thanks. You can go now, if you want."

"*Primero* we check the house."

They both scampered inside before I could say a word. I stepped out of the car, then reached into the back for Katherine.

"Did you hurt him?" I asked when she was standing on the sidewalk beside me.

She shook her head, but I didn't believe her.

"Come on."

Together we trudged up the stairs. I heard the boots of the Mexicans as they pounded through the house. It didn't sound like they'd found anybody, and they hadn't.

"Did you look in the closets?"

"*Sí, sí. Por todos lados.* Everywhere."

"The basement?"

"*Sí, allí también.*"

Buddy wasn't in the house. He wasn't anywhere in the backyard either.

"Where is he?" I demanded.

Katherine shook her head.

In the suddenly silent room, through the still-open front door, I heard the roar of a MUNI bus down on Balboa.

"Watch her," I said to the Mexicans, then rushed out to my car and drove straight to Payton Murphy's house.

CHAPTER
53

HE WASN'T HERE. I'd circled the house twice and hadn't found him. He couldn't have gotten inside. I tried all the doors and windows. Everything was locked.

I circled back to the front door and sat down on the steps. Maybe she *had* killed him. Maybe Buddy was gone.

"I'm sorry, Buddy," I said softly. "I'm sorry I let you down."

I sat there in silence a moment thinking of Buddy's easy smile and open heart, remembering the first time I'd met him wandering around the yard, looking lost.

The wind rustled the trees across the street, and in the distance a siren screamed. Then suddenly everything went quiet. In the silence I heard the distant shuffling sound of steps. I glanced down the street and saw a figure, a bulky, flat-footed figure, head down, hands deep in his pockets, trudging up the sidewalk thirty yards away. My heart missed a beat.

I jumped up. "Buddy?"

The figure's head whipped up. He hesitated, peering at me through the dark, then finally raised his hand and waved. "Ronnie Vee!" he shouted.

CHAPTER 54

SINCLAIR WALLINGFORD OPENED the door to his parents' house and grinned.

"I know who you are," he announced proudly. From behind him came the sounds of laughter and music. "You're Buddy's best friend, Blackie," he said, pointing. "And you're his other best friend, Ronnie Vee. I bet you're here for Buddy's birthday party."

"They certainly are, Sinclair." Nicole Wallingford, beaming, three-pronged metal cane in hand, walked laboriously but proudly to stand beside her stepson. "We're celebrating my emancipation from the wheelchair too," she announced, then invited us inside.

"Sinclair, why don't you take their gifts for Buddy and put them on the table with the others?"

Once he'd rushed back into the party, Nicole leaned heavily on her cane and said, "Thank you so much for coming. It means a lot to Buddy to have you here. Especially since his mother can't make it."

"Still in detox?" Blackie asked.

"She has three weeks left. Harry's brother has promised her work at his law firm. And Dr. Patel has offered the use of the cottage in back of her house until Sondra's ready for a place of her own."

"Sounds like you've been busy," I said. "Phoebe told me you and Harry talked to the D.A. and convinced him to drop the charges against me. Thanks."

"I believe he was leaning in that direction anyway," she said. It was a gracious lie, and all three of us knew it.

"How does Buddy feel about his new little brother?" I asked.

"I can't separate them. They always saw lots of each other at school and got along so well that we haven't had any difficulties at all. But just in case, Dr. Patel is on standby to help us out if we need her. I'm sure they'll both be fine."

As Blackie started toward the living room, Nicole asked me to wait. Blackie hesitated, then went ahead.

"Excuse me for bringing this up," Nicole said once we were alone, "but is there anything new regarding that poor, unfortunate girl?"

"She confessed to everything. I thought Philly Post told you."

"He did." She glanced down at the rich, burnished floor, then gazed up at me with suddenly grief-stricken eyes. "This may sound odd, but I was hoping for something, some bit of positive news, something . . . I don't—I don't know what. The only thing that keeps going through my mind is that she must have been in such a lot of pain to do those awful things. I just can't stop thinking about her."

Behind us, in the living room, Blackie said something, and Buddy's voice rose in laughter. Other voices joined in.

I smiled for a moment at the purity of the sound, then turned back to Nicole Wallingford and said, "You know what? Neither can I."

Match wits with the best-selling
MYSTERY WRITERS
in the business!

SUSAN DUNLAP

"Dunlap's police procedurals have the authenticity of telling detail."
—*The Washington Post Book World*

☐	AS A FAVOR	20999-4	$3.99
☐	ROGUE WAVE	21197-2	$4.99
☐	DEATH AND TAXES	21406-8	$4.99
☐	KARMA	20982-X	$3.99
☐	A DINNER TO DIE FOR	20495-X	$4.99
☐	DIAMOND IN THE BUFF	20788-6	$4.99
☐	NOT EXACTLY A BRAHMIN	20998-6	$4.99
☐	TIME EXPIRED	21683-4	$4.99
☐	TOO CLOSE TO THE EDGE	20356-2	$4.99
☐	PIOUS DECEPTION	20746-0	$3.99

SARA PARETSKY

"Paretsky's name always makes the top of the list when people talk about the new female operatives." —*The New York Times Book Review*

☐	BLOOD SHOT	20420-8	$5.99
☐	BURN MARKS	20845-9	$5.99
☐	INDEMNITY ONLY	21069-0	$5.99
☐	GUARDIAN ANGEL	21399-1	$5.99
☐	KILLING ORDERS	21528-5	$5.99

SISTER CAROL ANNE O'MARIE

"Move over Miss Marple..." —*San Francisco Sunday Examiner & Chronicle*

☐	ADVENT OF DYING	10052-6	$3.99
☐	THE MISSING MADONNA	20473-9	$4.99
☐	A NOVENA FOR MURDER	16469-9	$3.99
☐	MURDER IN ORDINARY TIME	21353-3	$4.99
☐	MURDER MAKES A PILGRIMAGE	21613-3	$4.99

LINDA BARNES

☐	COYOTE	21089-5	$4.99
☐	STEEL GUITAR	21268-5	$4.99
☐	SNAPSHOT	21220-0	$4.99
☐	BITTER FINISH	21606-0	$4.99

At your local bookstore or use this handy page for ordering:

DELL READERS SERVICE, DEPT. DS
2451 South Wolf Rd., Des Plaines, IL. 60018

Please send me the above title(s). I am enclosing $ _____
(Please add $2.50 per order to cover shipping and handling.) Send
check or money order—no cash or C.O.D.s please.

Dell

Ms./Mrs./Mr. _____

Address _____

City/State _____ Zip _____

DGM-1/95

Prices and availability subject to change without notice. Please allow four to six
weeks for delivery.